Praise for

Scott Rosberg did a fantastic job with his new book, *Ultimate Team Player*. He made me care deeply about each of the characters. I couldn't help but picture unselfish teammates I have known through the years while reading the scenes with Remington, the main character. Scott's ability to change character perspective and give a believable voice to each character was done well. As a coach myself, I kept hoping that the antagonist, Cade, would see the light, just like we do for certain kids that we coach. I could relate to Remington's fear of a romantic mis-step with his good friend Jenny, who he begins to have stronger feelings for as the story progresses. Scott's messages were clear and consistent throughout the book. Instilling a philosophy of unselfishness as the major focus in a fictional format is a strategy that works well for readers. I look forward to the next installment in his series. Well done, Scott!

—Bob Kuykendall, veteran high-school English teacher and wrestling coach

There is only one guarantee in any athletic season… it will not be perfect. There are going to be challenges. You can't put twelve or more 12- to-18-year-old players together for four months without some struggles. There will be issues with playing time, relationships, jealousies, and drama. In *Ultimate Team Player*, Scott Rosberg takes us on an insightful and entertaining, season-long, rollercoaster journey with a high-school basketball team. Readers who are players or coaches will recognize many of the same issues they have faced with their own teams and learn from how the players and coaches in the story dealt with them. If you are an athlete, coach, or parent of an athlete, you're going to love *Ultimate Team Player*.

—Bruce Brown, veteran coach and Founder/Director of Proactive Coaching

Praise for *Ultimate Team Player*

Ultimate Team Player's message of success through working together is timeless, applies to all areas of life, and is especially important in any "team" endeavor. That ability really is at the heart of competing like a true champion! I thoroughly enjoyed reading this book and found so many things that fascinated me. As a non-basketball player, it was interesting to learn about some of the detail and strategy involved in this sport. As a coach, I appreciated the care taken in showing the perspectives of the Head and Assistant Coaches, and the depth of thought they approached coaching with. As a fan, I loved following the action in the games, and could feel the tension of the moments. I loved it!"

—*Karl Norton, veteran hockey coach*

Scott Rosberg has written a book that is very difficult to put down. The closer I got to the last page, the less I wanted the book to end. Throughout the story, I became fully invested in the lives of its characters. I had hopes and wishes for all of them. I can't wait to read his next book to see if those wishes come to fruition. As a teacher, a middle-school basketball coach, and a pleasure reader, I will be recommending this book to my students, my teams, and my fellow readers. Go Remington!

—*Zack Knaff, teacher and middle-school basketball coach*

ULTIMATE TEAM PLAYER

Remington Reunites the Team

SCOTT ROSBERG

A REMINGTON ROBERTS NOVEL

LIVINGSTON, MONTANA

ULTIMATE TEAM PLAYER
Remington Reunites the Team
A Remington Roberts Novel

Scott Rosberg

Copyright © 2021
by Scott Rosberg and SlamDunk Success

All rights reserved. Except as permitted under the U.S. Copyright Act of 1976, no part of this publication may be reproduced, distributed, or transmitted in any form or by any means, or stored in a database or retrieval system, without the prior written permission of the publisher.

Print ISBN: 978-0-9961320-6-0
eBook ISBN: 978-0-9961320-7-7

Printed in the United States of America
Editing, Typesetting & Cover: Denis Ouellette

SlamDunk Success
P.O. Box 2062
Livingston, Montana 59047

www.SlamDunkSuccess.com

~~~ DEDICATION ~~~

For all the Remingtons out there trying to make their teams better, their businesses better, and their families better, this one is for you. We need more of you making the world a more selfless, better place for all of us to live in. Keep the team-first attitude alive and well in the world!

~~~ DISCLOSURE & DISCLAIMER ~~~

As happens with any author, much of what I wrote in this story was informed by my own experiences or by my wishing that they were real experiences. No writing is ever completely objective, as the people writing it are human beings with thoughts, feelings, experiences, and biases that are part of who they are. While the characters in here may have characteristics of people who I have known, observed, or heard of, none of them are based completely on any actual people. Rather, each is a combination of many different people I have known or they exhibit the characteristics of people that I have either known or imagined as being part of the human experience in some way. I imagine people reading this from all parts of the world might say something like, "Oh, that's just like So-and-So," without me having any clue who So-and-So is. Any similarity of characteristics, behaviors, and actions to any real persons is both a possibility that it was sparked by someone you know and coincidental at the very same time.

Chapter 1

"**Our number-one focus** has to be each other. If we are going to achieve the success we seek, that we believe we are destined for, we must all have a team-first attitude."

Coach Del Brooks, head basketball coach of Sacajawea High School in Discovery, Montana, looked around the locker room, making eye contact with each member of his basketball team. He locked in on senior shooting guard, Cade Clemons. An All-Conference player during his junior year, Cade was the most talented player on the team, but he was also the most selfish. Coach Brooks paused for a moment as he looked at Cade. Cade looked to the floor.

Del returned to looking around the room at other players and continued. "It's not enough that you are good. It's not enough that your skills are better than other guys' skills. You have to make sure that you use your own individual strengths and skills to help the team succeed."

He paused for a moment to gauge how well his message was landing. All eyes were locked in on him. "Each of you has your own individual strengths that you bring to this team. Some of you are great shooters, some attackers, some passers, some rebounders, some encouragers and supporters, some great practice players. You each possess certain skills that bring value to this team. And every one of those values is just as important as the other one.

"While the general public sees the scorer as the most important one," he said while glancing back at Cade, "the truth is that the different skills that each of you bring to this team are just as important as the scoring. Without the screen, the scorer doesn't get open. Without the pass, the scorer doesn't get the ball to be able to score. Whether it's ballhandling, rebounding, defensive pressure, being a great practice player pushing those who play more, unselfishly giving of yourself for the good of the team, we need each of you to do what you do best to become our best."

Junior point guard, Remington Roberts, was fixated on every word that Coach Brooks was saying. He loved that message. He loved being part of a team, giving of himself to the team, and doing all that he could to help the team. He loved the guys he played with on this team in particular.

Actually, that wasn't completely true. Remington struggled with Cade. He caught Coach Brooks's quick stop on Cade as he made his initial comment. He wondered if Cade was actually listening, but he doubted it. He had known and played with Cade way too long to believe Cade was buying any of it. But Remington had hope.

Del continued as he looked around the room. Players, coaches, and managers were all locked in on him. "Boys, I don't usually set specific win-loss and championship-types of goals. I think it's better to focus on actions and habits to create those actions. I have always thought that if we focus on being the best we can possibly be, by working the hardest that we are capable of working, and by setting goals along those lines, then the wins and losses will naturally follow."

Del paused for a moment and then continued. "However, we have an amazing opportunity in front of us this year. We have the type of team that can make it to the state tournament. Our school has not been there for some time. But this year, we have the talent to get there."

Many of the players were smiling at this comment. Del continued, "But we will only get there if we play the way I have been speaking of. So, I'm going to do something now that I have never done with you. I'm going to put a specific goal up on the board, and I'm going to leave it up there all year long, so that you will constantly be reminded of it. It's three little words, yet they will be the three biggest words of the year for this team."

Del turned around to face the white board. He picked up the red dry-erase marker and wrote, "Get to State" in the upper right corner of the board. He turned around and said, "Get to State." He paused, looked around the room, and then repeated it. "Get to State. Three words that will be a constant reminder to us of what is at stake if we do or if we don't play the way we need to play and the way we are capable of playing. Tonight, we start our quest to," and he pointed at the board, "Get to State."

Del looked around the locker room. He saw excitement and joy on the faces of the boys. They were about to explode. He yelled, "What are we gonna' do?!"

Chapter 1

The boys all yelled, "GET TO STATE!!"

"What?!"

"GET TO STATE."

"Again!"

The boys started chanting, "GET TO STATE! GET TO STATE! GET TO STATE!"

Del raised his hand to quiet them. "That's the passion and the fire you need to bring every night. Not every game night, but every practice, every team meeting, every single day that we are together. If you attack this season with that kind of intensity you will," he said, turning and pointing to the board again, "Get to State."

Del looked back at them, and said, "However, there is one more word we need to put up here. And this one is a much bigger word than the other three, not only in the size of the word, but in its importance to us achieving all that we want to achieve." He turned back around to the white board. Underneath "Get to State," he wrote in all caps—"TOGETHER."

He turned back around. "Boys, passion, excitement, and intensity are critical to our success and to our goal of getting to state. But if we don't do it," he pointed at the word on the board and continued, "TOGETHER, then it won't happen. We MUST be a together team if we are going to," pointing to the board again, "Get to State. Tonight's first practice is the first test of the season that you have. Are you ready? Have you put in the work in the off-season? Did you come in ready to go, in good shape, basketball shape, ready-to-run-your-butt-off shape? Are you ready to focus for two hours and take what you're told and apply it to your practice habits?"

Del paused again. He could see their understanding and recognition of what he was getting at. "Gentlemen, tonight is step one on a journey that we will be taking together for the next four months. The question is, 'Are YOU ready?' The answer awaits out on that court. Let's get out and get our pre-practice warm-up started. Everyone up and in here."

The team came into a tight group surrounding Coach Brooks. Del raised his right hand, and they all reached up and touched each other's hands. He noted Cade on the outside of the group, looking at the floor, with his hand barely up near the others, but he said nothing. Del said, "Together on three... 1, 2, 3," and they all yelled, "Together!"

Ideas to Consider:

- What is Coach Brooks' main message for his team in the locker room?
- Why does he feel it's important for his team to receive this message?
- Who does he feel needs to hear this message more than anyone else? Why?

Chapter 2

When the team broke their huddle and started towards the door, Del said, "Cade," loud enough for Cade and a couple of others to hear, but not so loud as to sound like he was scolding him.

"Yeah, Coach," Cade said.

Del let all the others make their way out the door before he turned to Cade. "You know how much I believe in you, right?" Cade nodded his head, but not in such a way that made it completely clear that he fully believed it. "Cade, you have as much skill and talent as anyone I have coached in my time here. You have worked very hard to become the player you have become, and you have the potential to be a very special player." Cade liked the thought of that.

"You have every opportunity to be one of the best we have had through here in a long time. I'm really excited for you and what could happen for you this year."

Cade smiled and nodded. "Thanks, Coach. I'm really excited, too."

Del said, "But here's the deal, Cade. Your individual skills and potential success can do great things for you. But there's a catch." Del paused a quick moment. "They will only do great things for you if they also do great things for us."

Cade looked a bit confused. Del continued. "I know how much you want to play in college. I know it's been your dream for a long time, and I know you would love to play D1. I also know that you haven't had any D1 schools looking at you yet, have you?"

Cade dropped his head and nodded, "No."

"I know how tough that's been on you. Do you know why no D1 schools have shown interest in you yet?"

Cade looked up and said, "I'm too short, too white, and too Montana."

"No, that's not it at all, Cade. In fact, that's an excuse. There's a lot of short, white guys playing D1 ball right now, some even from Montana. Always have been and always will be. That has nothing to do with D1 schools not looking at you. . . yet. No, the main reason why is we didn't win last year. We were only 5 & 15. Because of that, nobody knew about us, so nobody knew about you. I talked with a couple of college coaches occasionally during the season, but we just weren't on their radar. After the season we put together that video of your highlights, and that got you some attention from D2s and NAIA schools, so that's a start. But the only way you're really going to turn heads this year is if we start winning."

Del knew that he was hitting home with Cade. Like most good players, Cade felt he had NCAA Division 1 skills and felt he could play at that level if he was just given a chance. Del knew this and knew that he had to watch how he pushed Cade's buttons, so it didn't backfire and hurt the team. He had to be careful with this line of reasoning.

"Now understand that I'm not saying you have to do and be everything, Cade. Your skills are good enough that people will see what you are capable of and how good you are. The key is getting them to see you play. And one of the best ways for that to happen is for us to be winning, or at least competing, every night against every team.

Del paused for a moment to let his words sink in. He had given Cade similar messages the last two years, usually with little to no result. But this being Cade's senior year and having no D1 coaches showing any interest in him yet, Del thought that Cade might be a little more open to the message.

Del continued. "So, for you to have the success you seek and get the shot that you want to get, not only do you have to be the best you can be at your own individual game, but you also have to help raise the rest of us to be our best. The better you are AND the better we are, the better chance you have of getting noticed. Does that make sense?"

Cade nodded, "Absolutely, Coach. I get it. I need to be great, so we can be great."

Del tilted his head, "Well, yes and no. It depends upon what you mean by you 'being great.' If it means you're a great teammate, getting everyone else involved, contributing in a variety of ways offensively, while also being a lock-down defender, showing yourself to be coachable, focused, and a team-first player, absolutely. If you do those things, your being great will help lead to us being great."

Cade nodded his understanding. Del continued. "However, if by you being great you mean you need to score every time you touch it, and you need to handle the ball all the time and everyone needs to do what you want them to do and play off of what you want to do, no. That will get you nowhere and us nowhere. That will show you to be all about you only and not at all about your teammates and your team. While you may have some 'great' nights doing that, you will completely limit our chances of being as successful as we can be and your chances of achieving your dream of playing D1. Does that make sense?"

Del could see Cade was trying to figure out if he had just been scolded, praised, a combination of both, or neither of those. Cade finally said, "Yeah, Coach. I get it."

Del said, "Good. Cade, I want you to understand that no one is behind you more or more hopeful that you achieve your goals than me." Del knew that this might be hard for Cade to believe because of how things were between the two of them the prior year. Part of the reason the team struggled the prior year was because Cade had been all the things that Del had just mentioned as being problems. Cade never bought into Del's message. He felt he could just take over and do his own thing. It was a constant battle all season, and the team struggled on the scoreboard because of it. They also struggled in practice, in the locker room, on the bus, and everywhere else because of it. The team chemistry was horrendous, non-existent.

Del did not want a repeat of that this year, and he wanted Cade to understand the importance of not being that kind of player again. "I want you to get what you want to get. Because quite honestly, if you get what you want, I believe we will get what we want. You know why?" Cade looked intently at Del.

Del continued, "Because the only way you'll get what you want is if we get what we want. While you have a lot of control over how you play, it will take all of us playing well and having success for you to get the looks you seek. You will get what you want—a chance to play D1—if we get what we want—a chance to play in the state tournament. Do you understand that?

"Yeah, I think so."

Del felt Cade was getting it. "The better we are, the more success we have, the more people will be seeing us, the more coverage we will get, and the farther into the post-season we get, the more college coaches will hear about us. That means more college coaches will potentially be seeing you."

Del watched Cade's eyes to see if he was comprehending what Del was saying. Del continued, "Cade, you may not believe this, but I want you to achieve your dreams. I want you to get that chance to play D1. But I don't want that to happen at the expense of this team. In fact, I can't have the needs of this team come in second place to your needs. And understand, I would be saying that to ANYONE who has a shot like you do. It's just that this year, you are probably the only one with any kind of a shot like that."

Del knew Cade felt very highly of his own talents and abilities. He also knew Cade liked having his ego stroked often. Cade tried to hide that with an exterior of cool and an "I don't care" attitude. But Del knew that inside, Cade really liked all the attention he received.

"So what do you think?" Del asked. "Can you put the needs of the team first, so that we get the success we seek, so you can ultimately get the success you seek?"

"Absolutely, Coach." Cade replied. "I got this."

"Excellent!" said Del. "Get out there and get your warm-up going."

As Cade headed out the locker room door, Del thought, "We'll see. He seems to always say the right words, but his actions don't always follow suit. I hope he means it this time, cuz if he does, this could be a really special year... for all of us!"

Ideas to Consider:

- **What is one of Cade's biggest goals? Why could that be a problem for the team this year?**
- **How does Coach Brooks try to use that goal to help Cade see how it can help the team?**
- **What is Cade's reaction to Coach Brooks' comments?**

Chapter 3

As the team was warming up, Remington was shooting at a basket with Nick Bertucci and Tim Nelson, his best friends on the team. They were also juniors. Remington and Nick were the two best players in the junior class. Tim was more of a role player who gave everything he had to make his teammates better and never complained about anything. These three had been playing together since 5th grade, and they had played with the seniors all that time, too. Remington's dad, a coach himself for many years, had taken the boys to spring and summer tournaments during their 5th through 8th grade years. All of the boys in both classes bonded together really well through all those years—all except Cade.

Cade just had a way about him. He was nice for the most part, but he was stand-offish at times. He carried an aura that said, "I'm better than you. Don't even try to test me on it." Therefore, he didn't blend in well with the others. He didn't hang out with them. He went to many of the activities they all went to, but he was kind of just outside of their circle, no matter what was going on. From team huddles in games, to where they aligned themselves or sat in the locker room, to just hanging out as friends, Cade was always just to the outside.

Was it conscious? Did he truly feel like that about his teammates? It was hard for his teammates to know for sure, but they all felt it. As Remington, Nick, and Tim warmed up, Remington said, "Do you think any of what Coach said in there sunk into Cade at all?"

Nick responded, "Hell no! Are you kidding me? He won't put the team first. He hasn't in all of our years of playing with him. Why would he now? Just cuz Coach said so? Coach said that same stuff all last year and all summer and look how well that worked out."

Tim nodded his agreement with Nick and said, "Yeah, but did you hear Coach call Cade back in before we headed out here? What do you think that was all about?"

"I think it's Coach trying to do what Coach should have done better last year—jump on it early," said Nick. "If Coach would have actually had the guts to stop Cade from being so selfish last year, who knows what could have happened to us? We were good, a whole lot better than sub-.500."

Remington thought of how difficult last year was. He said, "I hope Coach is starting off on the right foot with him this year, so we don't have to deal with his crap anymore. I know it's probably wishful thinking, but I agree with Coach. We do have an amazing opportunity this year. But Cade needs to be on board with us if that's going to happen."

"No kidding," said Nick. "If he would ever pull his head out of his ass and actually play like he actually likes playing with us, this could be something special. We have more talent on this team than I've seen in quite a while."

Tim said, "You can talk to him all you want about getting to state if we do it together, but he won't care. He just cares that he gets his 20 every night. He doesn't care if we win."

"You know that's not completely true, Tim," said Remington. "He cares if we win. He gets pissed when we lose just like anyone else."

Nick responded, "No, Rem, it's not 'just like anyone else.' He gets pissed when we lose because he thinks it makes him look bad. Sure, he wants to win as much as anyone else, but just for the wrong reasons. He thinks if we don't win, he won't get college scouts to see him. He thinks if we don't win, it shows that he's not any good. So, then when we don't win, he blames us. He blames everybody else but himself."

"I guess you're right," said Remington. "But you know, if we could get him to see that when we win, he has a better chance at getting seen by scouts and being recruited, he might just start to buy in to the concept. I'm sure he thought he would have been recruited last year. If he had played like a good teammate and we would have won some more games, maybe he would have been. We need to get him to see that when he plays team ball, we have a better chance to win. When we have a better chance to win, he has a better chance to play in college. If we can get him to see that, maybe he'd be better to all of us."

"Two things about that," said Tim. "First, I'll only believe it when I see Cade actually being better to all of us. And second, how do you plan on getting him to do that?"

Remington thought for a moment. "I don't know for sure. I just know that if we can try to get him on board, you never know what might happen."

Nick couldn't resist, "Yeah well with the way he treated you in particular last year and this summer at tournaments, I don't know how much you're going to be able to get him to change. I still can't believe how hard he was on you—you of all people. You're like the best teammate and nicest guy on the team, and he still treated you worse than anybody."

"Maybe that's why he treated him worse than anybody," said Tim. "Remington is too nice. Rem, you gotta' step up into his face sometime and let him have it. You can't let him treat you like that this year, especially if you want him to act the way you're wanting him to act."

Cade had just come out of the locker room and was headed straight towards Remington, Nick, and Tim at the far end of the court. Remington had spoken to Cade throughout the fall in the school's hallways, cafeteria, and the classes they had together. It was as if none of what happened on the court last year or in the summer had ever happened. But that was Cade. He was actually a nice guy once you had him away from basketball. But once he got around the game, it was like a switch flipped.

As Cade approached, Remington wondered, "Okay, now what is he going to say to me?"

Cade stepped up a few feet away from him. "Hey, Rem. I just want you to know things are going to be different this year. I was a jerk last year and this summer. I'm done being that way. You're going to see a whole new me this year."

Remington couldn't believe what he was hearing, and he felt a tinge of hope. He said, "Sounds good, Cade. I just want us to have the best year we can. I think we could be really good this year. And if we all play together as a team, we can get to state. And if we can get to state, anything's possible, right?"

"Absolutely," said Cade. "We cool, then?"

"We cool," said Remington. They fist-bumped and Cade trotted off to shoot at another basket—alone.

Nick turned to Remington and Tim and said, "Yeah right. Like I said before, 'I'll believe it when I see it.'"

"I don't know," said Remington. "When have you ever seen or heard Cade do something like that before?"

"Uh, only every time he acts like a jerk and then feels bad about it," said Tim.

"Yeah, I guess you're right," said Remington. "That just felt different from those other times, though. At least, I hope something was different there this time."

Nick said, "I'm sure you do, Rem. We all do. We all want him to not be such a jerk. But since we've never seen it, I won't believe it until I see him being one." He paused and then said, "By the way. Look who he's shooting with."

Remington and Tim looked over at Cade shooting. "No one," said Remington.

"Exactly," said Nick.

Del Brooks blew his whistle and yelled "Rack 'em up!" indicating that practice was about to begin.

The boys came together in a circle around Del. He looked at all of them, looked around the gym, and said, "Boys, we just spent fifteen minutes talking about the kinds of things we need to do to become the team we want to become. But that was while we were sitting in a locker room. The locker room is an important place for a team. It is where we will spend a lot of time together getting ready for practices and games, hanging out, meeting, bonding. However, everything that we do to become a team in the locker room is done in one way—talking.

"But talking about what you want and actually doing it are two very different things. Between these lines and over on our team bench is where the rubber meets the road. We can sit in the locker room and talk all day and all night, but if we don't come out here and do what we say we're going to do and behave the way we say we're going to behave and perform the way we say we want to perform, all the talk in that locker room won't matter. In fact, all the talk in the locker room is actually worse if we don't come out here and do it because it means all our talk is just a bunch of lies.

"So if you truly want the kinds of things we talked about in there, and if you truly want the kinds of things that I believe you want and you're capable of getting, you need to prove it out here. You prove it to each other, to us, to your parents, and the fans. But most of all, you each have to prove it to yourself. Make sure that your words and thoughts and commitments are proven out here every night by your actions." Del looked around at everybody. "Get it?"

They all responded, "Got it."

"Good," said Del. "Let's get started. Cade and Billy, you two lead the stretch."

Ideas to Consider:

- What concerns do Nick, Tim, and Remington have about Cade?
- How does Remington differ in his feelings than Nick and Tim? Where do their feelings come from?
- What concerns do Nick and Tim have about Remington and Cade's relationship?
- Have you ever had a player who you had similar concerns about to the concerns that Coach Brooks, Nick, Tim, and Remington have about Cade? Why? What did you do to try to get that player to change? What could you have done differently?

Chapter 4

As they went through their stretching routine, Remington was lost in thoughts about his conversation with Nick and Tim a few moments before. He knew they were right. While one of his greatest attributes was his selflessness and his easy-going, positive demeanor, it also was one of his greatest weaknesses as a leader. He just didn't like to confront people that needed confronting. And Cade needed a lot of confronting. But Cade was not easy to get along with when he got into his overly competitive mode, so Remington let him be. When Cade lashed out at Remington for things that Cade felt Remington did wrong, Remington would just turn and head back down the court and never confront him. Sometimes Remington's teammates would tell Cade to shut up, but Remington rarely did.

As his own game started blossoming in tournament games during the past summer, Remington started to stand up for himself more. He started having higher scoring games, getting the ball to teammates for easy buckets more, and handling the point guard duties more, thereby "running the show" more. While the team flourished when he did that, Cade didn't like it. Cade saw it as Remington starting to horn in on his territory as top dog on the team. He didn't like that Remington was having success and getting a lot more attention, so he lashed out even more than he had over the last year.

But as the summer went on, with his game rising, Remington started feeling a little more confident in standing up to Cade. In the last game of the summer, Remington was going off. Driving the lane and scoring, dishing to open teammates when help defenders collapsed on him, and knocking down three 3-pointers in the first half, Remington was without a doubt, the best player on the floor. At halftime, Coach Brooks talked about how well the team was playing together. He highlighted how Remington was setting a nice tone with his drives and finishes or kick-outs to open shooters. He then said, "Let's keep feeding off that and keep this thing rolling. Keep attacking, Rem, and good things will continue to happen."

Chapter 4

After they broke the huddle and headed out to the court to get some warm-up shots, Cade headed straight to Remington. Once they were out of earshot of everyone else, Cade lashed out at Remington. "Why don't you pass the ball, you frickin' ball hog?"

Uncharacteristically, Remington shot back at Cade. "Are you kidding me? You haven't thrown a pass to a teammate all game. Hell, I don't think you've passed it all tournament! Shut the hell up, and start playing team ball."

Cade stepped up into Remington's face. "Don't you ever talk to me like that again, or I will beat the crap out of you. You are nothing. This team is nothing without me. Don't you ever forget that!"

Remington was shaken. He walked over and grabbed a ball and started shooting, but his mind was far away from being focused on getting his shooting rhythm ready for the second half. While he felt good that he had stood up to Cade, he was really bothered by how Cade talked back to him. Truth be told, he was scared. He knew Cade was stronger than he was, more aggressive than he was, and was enough of a jerk that he wouldn't put it past him to "beat the crap" out of him.

In the first ten minutes of the second half, Remington played with much less strength and confidence. He deferred a lot more to Cade than he had in the first half and in the last couple of tournaments. He reverted back to the player he had been the prior year whenever Cade was on the floor with him. He stopped attacking and shooting, only looking to get the ball to his teammates, especially Cade.

Del called a timeout and told him to get aggressive and attack. He did a couple of times, both with success—a finish at the rim and a kick-out to Nick for a three. But as they were headed down the floor to play defense, Cade yelled at him, "Get me the ball." Remington just turned and faced up to guard his man.

On the opponents' next shot, Remington got the rebound and started dribbling up the right sideline. Cade was streaking down the left side of the court and started angling toward the lane. Remington saw him, looked toward the right corner, and rifled a no-look bullet pass right between two defenders that hit Cade perfectly in the hands. It was one of those passes that makes people say, "WOW!" Everyone on the floor and the bench started howling and high-fiving, except for Cade and Remington. Remington stared

15

at Cade, waiting for "Nice pass" comment that Del made his players say to each other in those moments. Jogging back down the court, Cade never even looked at Remington. "What a jerk," thought Remington. "Last time you get a pass like that from me."

A few possessions later, Remington received an outlet pass on the left wing from Nick. Just like the last time, Cade streaked up the court and was ahead of the defense. Remington took three dribbles, faked like he was going to pass it ahead to Cade, and dribbled into a pull-up 3-pointer. Nothing but net. Nick high-fived Remington as he came back down the court. Cade made a bee-line towards Remington. "Pass the ball! I was wide open."

"Not until you thank me for the last pass, Cade," Remington said with a smile. He was feeling good about his game again, back in the mode he needed to be in to play his best. This was too good to let Cade's attitude drag him down. He was having fun playing again. The rest of the game he got the ball to his teammates in places all over the court. He even passed to Cade one time when Cade had come around a screen and was open under the basket. Remington threw the bounce pass through the tightest of windows— right between his defender's legs—and Cade caught it for an easy lay-up. "Bout time," said Cade as they ran back down the floor.

"I didn't throw that for you, Cade," said Remington. "I threw that for me. I wanted to see if I could do it. Too bad you could never throw a pass like that."

The ball had rolled away out of bounds after Cade's basket, so there was a momentary break before the other team threw it in and brought it up the court. Amazingly, Remington actually moved closer to Cade, so he could continue his commentary to him. "I know you couldn't have thrown that pass to save your life. That's because you never throw a pass unless it's flashy and makes you look what you think looks good. But it doesn't. You just look like a selfish hot dog, which is exactly what you are. Get your head out of your ass and start playing team ball, Dude. You might actually have fun because we might actually win."

Cade wanted to come back at Remington with all kinds of comments, but he couldn't. First, the other team was now entering the front court with the ball, so he had to play defense. But second, he couldn't think of anything to say. Remington had him. And it was the first time that Cade felt that way with Remington in all of his years of knowing him. "How could he talk to me that way? He never talks to me like that. I'll show him." But those were only thoughts. They never came out of his mouth.

The game ended with Sacajawea winning by 12. Remington led all scorers with 21 points, to go with 8 assists. He had come into his own during this tournament, but this game took him to new places. While he and everyone else always knew he had the ability to play that way, he had not allowed himself to step up and take over like that. He didn't want to be seen as a ball-hog. He wanted to please and be a good teammate. But in this game, he finally realized that the variety of skills that he possessed meant that in order to be the best teammate he could be, he needed to use ALL of those skills, which meant that sometimes he would shoot more than his teammates.

That game also took him to new places with regards to his demeanor. He finally stood up to Cade. He finally didn't back down and let Cade dictate for him how he would play. He knew he had a long way to go with this and that there would be more confrontations to come. Cade was just wired that way. He couldn't let Remington have any of the spotlight, much less ALL of it.

So Remington knew this day was just a small step on that journey. But he also knew it was a big step for him. He just needed to be prepared for those moments in the future when similar things would happen. He knew he needed to be ready to stand up to Cade again at some point during the season. But would he? Only time would tell. For now, he was just enjoying the moment and this newfound feeling that he had.

Ideas to Consider:

- **How did Cade treat Remington in the summer? How did Remington usually react? What did he do differently in the final game?**
- **How would you deal with Cade if he was on your team?**

Chapter 5

When Del told his team how special he thought the season could be, he meant it. He knew there was talent on this team, and when they played well together, they could be really tough to stop. Other than Cade, there were some other talented players. In fact, depending on who you asked, some felt that a couple of the boys were just as good, if not better than, Cade. Former and current coaches who knew the game, understood individual skills as well as team dynamics, and who had seen these boys grow up playing together often considered Cade as the second or third best of the bunch. They felt that he was probably the most talented individual player, but because of his selfishness and how much it hurt the team, he was actually not the overall best player.

One of those former coaches was Jim Turner. Jim had coached at Sacajawea High for the years between Del's dad coaching the team and Del coaching the team, and for a while, he had carried on the success that Del's dad had while coaching there. While they had not had the same level of success in Jim's last couple of years coaching, the program was in good shape when Del took over for him.

"Sure, Cade's got talent," Jim told Del one day while watching the players play in an open gym. "The problem is he doesn't care about his teammates, so he takes all that talent and selfishly uses it for his own good. But he actually hurts himself by doing that. He can't get good looks because defenses just key on him."

Jim continued, "I think Billy T might be as good as Cade skills-wise. And I know that Remington is just flat-out better than Cade. His skills are off-the-charts good. He just hasn't shown yet what he can do in games when he takes over because he is such a great teammate and people-pleaser. When he starts to take over, look out." Jim paused and then added, "The best thing about both of them, though, is that they focus on using their abilities to help the team win. You just don't ever see Cade do that."

Chapter 5

The "Billy T" that Jim was referring to was Billy Thompson. He was another senior who had always had a somewhat chilly relationship with Cade. They had been the two best players in their class growing up. As much as Billy wanted to be better friends with Cade, Cade was so competitive and jealous of Billy's skills, that he would never completely open up to become good friends with him. Cade always had to be better than Billy, and then Billy often felt that he had to do the same thing. This individual competitiveness put a crimp in their relationship. Billy hoped their senior year would be different, but he didn't have much faith.

Del's assistant coaches had differing opinions about who the best players were, mainly because the two of them were quite different from each other. The freshman coach, Braden Larson, was a former player at the school who had stayed in town working after graduation. He had been a good player, but just not good enough to be recruited to play in college. He ended up not going to college, so he never left town. He bounced around different jobs, mainly waiting tables and bartending at local restaurants. He loved the game and wanted to stay involved in some way, so three years ago in his third year out of high school, Braden decided to apply for the freshman position when it came open. While he was raw in terms of knowledge of the game and of coaching in general, he made up for it by being a hard worker and someone who would open the weight room, supervise open gyms, and take the kids to tournaments in the summer. Braden saw players the way he had seen them as a player himself. He focused on their skills and talents more than anything else. In his mind, Cade was by far the best player in the program. It was almost as if he didn't notice Cade's attitude issues.

The JV coach, Kevin Nixon, was at the other end of the coaching spectrum from Braden. Kevin reminded Del of his dad. Kevin had been a coach for over twenty years and a head coach for fifteen of them. His knowledge base and understanding of the game were excellent. In fact, in moments when Del doubted himself, he would often think, "Kevin should be coaching this team. He knows way more basketball than I do, maybe than I ever will."

While Del was confident in his own abilities, he just had moments of doubt, frustration, and confusion that would lead him to wonder if he was cut out to handle it. He didn't know if every coach felt this way at times, but his dad said that he had done that on almost a yearly basis, and most of the coaches he knew said the same thing. As Del thought about Kevin, he thought, "He just always seems to know what to say and do it in just the right way at just the right moments." Kevin was good for Del, and Del was grateful to have him on his staff.

Del was especially grateful to have Kevin there the prior year. Del's dad had passed away unexpectedly from a heart attack right before school started that year. It was a gut punch unlike anything Del had ever experienced. His dad was his best friend, and he was his closest confidant when it came to coaching. While Jim Turner was also a great help, Jim was no longer coaching, so he was not around all that much. But Del's dad was always ready to drop whatever he was doing and talk coaching with him. For the most part, Kevin was the same way for Del. Kevin was always willing to talk and help out in any way he could. After Del's dad died, having Kevin there was a great relief for Del.

As for Kevin, there was good reason why he wasn't the head coach at Sacajawea or anywhere else. He had burned out on coaching a few years before. He had a very successful teaching and coaching career at a few different schools around the state, the last one being at Colter High School, about 30 minutes east of Discovery. However, he had grown tired of the grind and being "the man in charge" and all the garbage that came with that. Eventually, the parents added to his frustration, too, and he decided he'd had enough. He resigned his coaching position, but he stayed in his math position because he still enjoyed teaching kids.

But after a couple of years of that, Kevin decided he needed a clean break from all of it, so he went into the private sector, getting what he called "a real job" selling real estate. While he did okay selling real estate, he found it to be fairly cutthroat. He grew tired of it after three years.

He also missed teaching and coaching. He especially missed the kids, who he always felt kept him young, energized, and on his toes. So when he saw an ad in the *Colter Sun* newspaper in early May for a math teaching position at Sacajawea High School over in Discovery for the next year, he was intrigued. Kevin had always liked the town of Discovery when he and his family would drive over to eat there or they would stop there on their way to the western part of the state. Discovery was a quaint little town with a combination of art galleries, bars, fly fishing shops, and eclectic boutiques and restaurants that gave it a funkiness that he liked a lot.

Kevin had also followed the basketball teams at Sacajawea for years. He had coached against Mason Brooks a few times before Mason resigned and then against Jim Turner a couple of times, as well. They were good guys and good coaches, and Kevin was always impressed with how hard their kids played, but also how poised, disciplined, and classy they were. Kevin's Colter teams always had superior talent to Sacajawea's teams. After all, Colter High was over three times the size of Sacajawea, so Colter's talent pool was far greater. And Kevin's teams were always some of the best in their AA classification, the largest in the state, so they always had a distinct advantage over a Class A school like Sacajawea. Still, Sacajawea always battled them hard, never backing down or showing any fear playing against the much bigger school. One time, Sacajawea even pushed Colter into overtime before finally succumbing.

Kevin quickly grew accustomed to teaching at Sacajawea High. He loved the kids he taught, the staff he worked with, and in general, the whole vibe around the school. He was so glad to be back teaching. While he had chosen not to coach during his first year there, he still attended sporting events. In the fall, he went to football, volleyball, and soccer games to watch his students play. As he sat in the stands that first year, the old coaching bug started gnawing at him ever so slightly. When the winter season hit and he was watching basketball games, he started really missing the coaching. He started stopping in to watch practices after school for a few minutes at a time before heading home. Soon, he was staying a half hour and sometimes an hour watching, taking mental notes on players, drills, strategies, and things he would like to try and things he would do differently if he were coaching. He went to every home game the basketball team played that first year and a few of the road games.

Kevin liked what he saw from Del and how he coached. He felt Del had taken a lot of his dad's characteristics, but he was also adding his own into the mix. He noticed a sophomore boy on the JV team named Cade Clemons. He could see that Cade was either the best player or the second-best player, with another sophomore named Billy Thompson being the other one. Kevin was impressed with Cade and Billy, but he saw some things in each of them that needed to be dealt with.

Billy had a tendency to try to drive too much when the opening wasn't there, causing him to force shots at bad times. He also seemed to be lost defensively, especially when the coach switched from one defense to another. Cade fit a stereotype of a "me-first" player. He was obviously very skilled, but he focused all of his abilities on himself, instead of on his team.

He would force shots that were not good shots, while he had teammates open in much better spots. When his teammates would take good open shots and miss, he would yell at them to pass the ball.

The brunt of many of Cade's negative comments was often Remington Roberts. Remington and Nick Bertucci were the only two freshmen who were playing up on the JV team. Kevin immediately saw why they were there, especially Remington. While Cade and Billy were the two best, most-skilled players on the team, Kevin saw things from Remington that made him think, "I'd love to coach THAT kid. He could become the best of the whole bunch."

The JV coach at the time was another former player named J.T. Calloway. This often happened in small towns. The coaching staff might consist entirely of people who had graduated from the school, and that was the case with the staff at Sacajawea High. Kevin had heard that J.T. had been a good player for Jim Turner, but a player somewhat similar to Cade. From Kevin's perspective, it seemed that J.T. rarely said anything to Cade about his behavior, and he never took him out of the game after one of his outbursts. In huddles, while J.T. was talking to the team, Cade would often be at the end of the five guys sitting on the bench looking out at the crowd or at the floor. He rarely paid attention. If he wasn't one of the players playing in the game during the timeout, he would not stand in the circle behind J.T. and listen to what J.T. was telling the 5 players who were playing at that time. He would usually be outside the circle, again, looking around the gym or talking to one of the managers.

Kevin did not like what he was seeing from Cade, and he thought, "If I had that kid, it would be a whole lot different for him." Then he would think, "And for me." Cade was one of the kinds of players that made Kevin have a love-hate relationship with coaching later in his career. When he was young and full of energy and enthusiasm for it, he loved coaching the players like Cade. He saw them as wild, untamed thoroughbreds. They had so much to offer that if he could tame them a bit and show them the right way to run for the good of the team, they could really help the team succeed and have a whole lot of fun along the way.

But as he grew older, the Cades of the world wore him down. They were a constant battle, and he eventually stopped wanting to fight it. Plus, they usually had parents that made it obvious why they behaved the way they did. That meant Kevin had to not only deal with the player, but he had to deal with the parents, too. It was a lose-lose situation, and it played a key role in Kevin deciding to hang up his whistle a few years back.

But sitting there in those stands watching, Kevin started itching to get back into coaching. So when J.T. Calloway resigned in the spring to take a job at a small school in the western part of the state, it opened up a spot on the staff. Kevin talked to Del about it, and Del was excited to have Kevin apply. Del had liked talking hoops with Kevin when they had done so throughout the year, and he could tell Kevin could be a great asset to the program and a great help to Del himself.

In their first year together, Kevin made a great impact, especially on Del. He lived up to Del's hopes for where he could help with the program. Del was grateful that things had come together the way they did. The team itself took steps in the right direction with Cade and Billy immediately making an impact on the varsity as juniors, becoming two of the best players in the conference. Remington and Nick made big impacts, too, as sophomores. They started the year out swinging between the JV and varsity teams. However, because of the impact they were making in the quarters they were playing on the varsity, after Christmas, Del put them on the varsity full-time.

While Del knew he should have done a better job of corralling Cade and making him more of a team player that year, the team took positive steps in terms of improvement and wins. With the addition of Remington and Nick, the strong individual skills of Cade and Billy, and the seniors who accepted their roles as solid role players, things were moving in a nice direction. Even though the team struggled to turn their skills and efforts into wins, things were looking up as that season came to a close.

Now with this new season just getting under way and his staff having a year under their belts together, Cade and Billy now seniors, Remington and Nick juniors, and a strong group of players around them, Del was looking forward to taking the next big steps as a program this year.

Ideas to Consider:

- **Most observers of the Sacajawea team would say Cade is the best player. Why does former coach Jim Turner feel that Cade might not be the best player on the team?**
- **What are some differences between Braden Larson and Kevin Nixon? Where do these differences come from?**
- **How can Kevin help Del?**

Chapter 6

As the first practice moved along, Del got more and more excited. Already the boys were clicking together. For a first day, they were quite crisp. They had put a lot of time into improving in the off-season, and most of them had been to all the open gyms in October. More importantly, they looked like they were having fun together. While they were busting their butts working hard, there were smiles on faces all over the gym. Even Cade was smiling and talking with the other guys. Had Del's words actually meant something to Cade? Of course, Del knew it was too early to tell, but he had hope.

As the boys made their way through the drills, they were constantly talking to each other, helping each other out with praise and encouragement. The older boys would shout positive words of encouragement to the younger boys, and at times, they would be explaining things to them.

Del loved what he was seeing because this was something that he always preached to his teams. "I am not the only leader here. Coach Larson and Coach Nixon are not the only leaders. Our captains are not the only leaders. Each of you has the capability and the green light to lead at any time. And the most important ways you lead are with your actions and your encouragement of your teammates. This is especially true with you juniors and seniors. Help the freshmen and sophomores. Increase and speed up their learning curve by showing them how we do things. The sooner they learn what it means to be a Wolves Basketball player, the sooner we all start to have even more success."

Last year, Cade had been a paradox with regards to this concept. Del would often see and hear him talking to younger players offering pointers. Del would get excited when he would see this. "Maybe he's starting to get it, starting to see the value of his teammates and making sure they are successful, too," Del would think. But then as he would make his way over near Cade to listen to what he was saying, so often the comments revolved around

Cade and how his teammate could and should be doing things to help get Cade the ball in prime scoring positions. Del realized that, while Cade was establishing relationships with the younger players, it seemed as if his sole purpose in doing so was to benefit himself, not the team.

But at this first practice, as he wandered around watching drills and listening to kids talk to one another, he heard Cade truly encouraging younger players, trying to help them improve *their* games, not his. He even heard him doing that with juniors and fellow seniors. It seemed like Cade really wanted to help them get better. Once again, Del found himself excited by what he was hearing, yet cautious about it, too. He knew it was just the first night.

Probably every high school basketball player in America did all the right things on the first night of the year. They all wanted to make the team by impressing their coaches, so their effort, attention, concentration, and commitment to one another were at their highest. Del knew this would be the case for the first few nights, and then the drop-off would probably occur. It was natural. However, one of Del's biggest goals this year was to see if he could minimize that drop-off and keep the kids focused on maintaining this level of practice performance throughout the year. He knew it was a tall task, but he also knew it could pay dividends if he could get them to do it.

For the rest of the practice the players and coaches maintained the high pace that had been established from the start. The coaches were pleased, and the players seemed pleased, too. In the post-practice huddle, when Del asked if anyone had anything to say, Remington spoke up saying, "Great effort, Guys. That was the best first practice I've been a part of in three years here."

Del nodded his agreement, and then Cade said, "Absolutely. If we keep this up for every practice, we could become something really special. Let's keep bringing it like that every night." Again, Del got a little tingle, hearing a comment like that from Cade.

As they broke the huddle, Del noticed Cade walking next to Remington as they headed toward the locker room. He caught the tail end of their conversation. Cade said, "Great job, Rem. You were right. That was a great first practice. That was fun."

Remington said, "Yeah. Everyone was bustin' their butts and yelling and encouraging. I haven't heard it or seen it like that before. That was a blast."

Chapter 6

Cade said, "Absolutely. And man, your jumper was wet! You were killing it out there tonight," as he reached up and high-fived Remington. Remington couldn't believe what he was hearing. Cade actually seemed to be excited for Remington to be scoring. That was something totally new.

Del also heard it and couldn't believe his ears either. Cade had never said anything like that to one of his teammates, especially Remington. While Del didn't want to get too excited over what he was hearing, he couldn't help but be somewhat excited over something he had been preaching to Cade for four years, yet had never seen or heard from him before. "If we can only keep this going," he thought.

Del's excitement level took another leap when he walked into the locker room. As he turned the corner around a bank of lockers, he saw Cade high-fiving Nick, then Mike, then Billy, and then each player in that row of lockers. To each one he said something like, "Great job out there tonight. Let's keep that going every night." Again, Del couldn't believe what he was seeing and hearing, and again, he got more excited. He walked into the coaches' office where Braden and Kevin were already sitting down and talking about practice.

Del said, "Did you guys see that?"

"Unbelievable, huh?" said Kevin.

Braden said, "What are you talking about?"

Del closed the door and said, "Cade just went around the room and high-fived every kid and said something positive either about the practice or about something the kid did. I've never seen that from him before, and I didn't think I would ever see something like that from him."

Kevin said, "Maybe your little pre-practice talk with him made an impression. Maybe this is the year he finally gets it and starts being the teammate he needs to be."

"I've been thinking the same thing," said Del. "The whole practice he seemed like a different kid. I know it's just the first night, so we need to be really careful how excited we get about it, but I've NEVER seen him act this way. Let's hope he not only got the message, but that he liked it and that he likes how it feels to be this way."

Kevin said, "We need to keep pounding that message into him. Well, not just him, but the whole team. But of course, he is the one who needs it the most. If we can keep the message in front of him, he has a chance. But we also need to keep rewarding him when we see him showing that he not only got the message, but that he believes it and that it matters to him. We'll get whatever we reward, not just with Cade, but with everyone. We'll also get whatever we tolerate and settle for, so we need to make sure we don't tolerate anything less than their best efforts and attitudes. They need to hear us constantly praising them when they are doing things the right way. And Cade has to be at the top of our list for doing that cuz the more he hears it and buys in, the more they will all be rewarded."

Del loved the way Kevin talked. He had a way of deciphering situations as they were and then explaining them and focusing on how to make them the best they could be. Of course, coaching all the years he had coached sure was a part of it. But there was something else about him that Del liked so much. He just had a way about him that Del had not seen with a lot of other coaches. His whole focus was on helping all kids have a great experience and making sure that all kids were beacons of integrity, effort, and team-first attitudes. He talked the talk, walked the walk, and made sure that the kids did the same.

Ideas to Consider:

- What was Coach Brooks' message to the team about leadership? How do you define "leadership"? What makes a great leader?
- How was Cade different in this practice and afterwards than at other times in the past?
- What does Kevin Nixon mean when he says, "We'll get what we reward," and "We'll also get whatever we tolerate and settle for."?

Chapter 7

Over the first couple of weeks of practice, the coaches saw more of the same. Yes, there were lapses in intensity and execution, but overall this was the kind of start that the coaching staff and the team were hoping for. The freshmen had split from the varsity and JV teams a week-and-a-half ago. Braden said they had done well at carrying on the same levels of effort and attitude that had been established in the first few days with the older kids. The JV and varsity continued to practice in much the same way they had those first few days, and when the JV would break off from the varsity and work on their own at the other end of the gym, Kevin noticed there was a high level of intensity that he didn't see last year. He was excited.

Del noticed it with his varsity team, too. He noticed it most in the communication and body language. Everyone seemed to talk more this year, both on the court and off. Heads were held a little higher, chests out a little more, and there was a lot more touching—the kind of touching that high school boys do with one another in the company of friends—high fives, jabs to the ribs, good-natured two-hand shoves to the shoulders.

More than anything, there were smiles and laughs. Del could see a palpable difference in the facial expressions of the team this year. Everyone seemed to smile more. The personalities on the team were such that this was bound to happen. Remington was a kid who always seemed to have a smile on his face. But Billy, Nick, Tim, and the rest of boys just seemed to be smiling a lot more than last year. While losing like they did last year will take the smiles off of faces, this year it felt like the team truly liked each other and enjoyed each other's company.

Most amazing of all was Cade. He, too, was joining in on it. This had not been like him in his previous three years. He had always been on the fringe, never joining in with the rest of the boys in their locker room, court, hallway, or bus behavior. He just didn't seem to care to be around them all that much. But this year, he was in there with them. Of course, he was still the old Cade at times, but he was different enough that it was noticeable. Del hoped it would continue. He knew that teams that get along off the court have a tendency to get along on it, and the more they get along, the better chance they have of playing well and winning.

Other people noticed a change, too. Jenny Jones was a girl that Remington had grown up with, and the two of them were best friends. Jenny was also a junior, and she and Remington lived around the corner from each other. They had become friends instantly when Remington moved into the neighborhood after fourth grade. While many boys at that age see girls as having "cooties," Remington never felt that way. He never bought into the whole "girls are bad" thing that some boys do. He immediately started doing things with Jenny. As they grew up, they continued to become closer. While they were not boyfriend and girlfriend, they might just as well have been. Neither of them dated anyone else, and they were always hanging out together. Jenny knew Remington as well as any of his teammates, probably even better.

As Remington and Jenny were walking through the hall at school one day, Cade walked by them. Remington happened to be wearing a Hawaiian shirt this day, one of his favorite shirts. While he loved this shirt and didn't care what people thought about him wearing it, he was self-conscious of it around Cade. That's because he was self-conscious of just about everything when he was around Cade. Cade had a negative effect on him, especially after last summer. But Remington's response in the final game of the summer, and the way Cade had been treating him this year and at practice so far had Remington feeling a little different. Still, he wondered how Cade would react to Remington wearing such a loud shirt.

Before Remington could say anything to him, Cade said, "Hey, Rem. Looking good, Dude! I love that shirt! Where'd you get it?"

Remington was not prepared for that, and he stammered a moment. "Uh, well, it is a Hawaiian shirt, Cade, so you know…"

Cade smiled and said, "No way? You went to Hawaii? When?"

Remington said, "I'm just kidding, Dude. I got it at the Goodwill. It's where all the fashion-conscious, upscale people in Montana shop."

They both laughed, and Cade turned to Jenny and said, "Jenny, how can you stand being seen with this guy?"

Chapter 7

She said, "Yeah, it's a tough job, Cade, but somebody's got to do it. If I didn't, who else would?" All three of them laughed and Cade started to walk away.

He said, "All right. Good to see you guys. See you at practice, Rem."

"Yeah, see you at practice, Cade."

As Jenny and Remington turned and continued down the hall, she said, "What the heck was that? I've never seen Cade be so nice to you. What do you think has gotten into him?"

"I don't know," said Remington. "Maybe it was Coach Brooks' talk to him at the start of the season. Whatever it is, I like it a whole lot more than the way it used to be. We'll see how long it lasts, though."

"Have a little faith, will ya'?" she asked. "Maybe this is the new Cade. Maybe he will be like this all year."

"I hope so," said Remington. "It's so much better not having to worry about Cade blowing up and being a jerk at any given moment. He's actually a really nice guy. But the moment he gets into "basketball mode," as I call it, he becomes a different person. It's a Jekyll and Hyde kind of thing."

"Well, maybe this is the year that Dr. Jekyll controls Mr. Hyde," Jenny said.

"I sure hope so," said Remington. "Not only will I enjoy it more, but we will be a much better team if he does."

"God, Rem, is that all you think about is basketball and what's good for the team? You can't go two minutes without somehow sticking in something about basketball or team or being good teammates into a conversation. Don't you ever turn it off?"

A little embarrassed, Remington said, "Uh, I don't know. I guess not. I just love basketball so much. I love being on a team and everyone working together and all of us striving to win and be the best we can be. I love that more than just about anything in the world."

Jenny looked back at the ground as he said that. While they had grown up together and had always been good friends, as they continued to grow up, Jenny had started seeing Remington in a little different light. They weren't romantic in any way, but she had started to have feelings for him like that in a small way. She had never really felt this way about anyone, but now it was happening to her with him. She wondered if he felt anything like that about her.

When Remington said what he said about loving basketball so much, it hurt a little bit. She knew basketball was his life, but she wanted him to think of her a bit like that, too. She hoped that someday he would be interested in her as more than just friends, but she knew better than to even consider bringing that up during the basketball season. She knew he had one focus at that time. She also liked him so much and knew how much basketball meant to him that she didn't want to do anything to screw that up for him. She figured that maybe they could talk about that other stuff after basketball season. Right now, she just said, "All right, Rem, I gotta' get to English. I'll see ya' later. Have a great practice!"

Remington said, "Thanks, Jenny. I'll see ya' later."

As he walked away from Jenny and headed to his math class, he thought about her. He wondered if she felt at all about him the way he had started feeling about her. While they had grown up together as good friends, as they had gotten older, he started seeing her a little differently. She had become one of the prettier girls in the school. As a soccer player, she was in great shape and had a very toned, athletic body. He had become attracted to her physically, but he had never expressed or even hinted to her that he felt that way. She had always been his best friend, and he didn't want to ruin that. Also, she had never indicated that she had any feelings for him, so he didn't dare say anything about it to her.

Someday maybe he would bring it up or try to feel out whether or not she might be interested in him in that way, but for right now, being best friends was good. He could talk with her about anything. She put him at ease when he needed it and made great moments even better. Nobody understood him better than Jenny, and he understood her that way, too. She was the best friend he could have ever hoped for. He was so glad that she was in his life.

Ideas to Consider:

- How is Cade treating Remington away from the court? Is this important for teammates to do, or does it only matter how they handle themselves on the court, field, mat, track, pool, etc. together?
- Who is Jenny Jones? What is the relationship between Remington and her like? What is the irony of how they are each feeling about one another?

Chapter 8

Sacajawea's **first two games of the season** were at the Tip-Off Tournament in Butte. Del liked playing in the Tip-Off tournament, for it provided good competition from teams in the western part of the state that they would not see during the season. It was a nice way to iron out some kinks before starting their conference season the following weekend.

The teams they were set to play were Bitterroot and Two Medicine. Their first game would be against Bitterroot. Bitterroot returned three starters from last year's team, and the word was they had a very good sophomore. They were a big team, with one player standing 6' 6," another at 6' 5," and another at 6' 3". Sophomore Brian Jackson was the second tallest player for Sacajawea standing at 6' 3½". But he was a wing player, not a thick post player, so they would struggle matching up with Bitterroot's size.

Del's plan was to wear down Bitterroot by running, pressing, and trapping them all over the floor. He knew they would give up their share of layups off their gambles, but his goal was to have those big boys tired in the 4th quarter. He also knew that ball handling was always suspect in the early part of the season, so turnovers could play a key role. If they pressed them all over the court, they could create turnovers, which could lead to a lot of fast break baskets for the speed players from Sacajawea. If they could be close late, Del liked their chances.

The game was a back-and-forth affair in the first quarter. The boys were sharing the ball well, and a lot of what the coaches had seen in the first weeks of practice was on display on the court. They communicated well, looked to the open man often, and found each other cutting to the basket. Nobody was dominating the basketball, and everyone was working well together. As they came to the bench at the end of the first quarter with the score tied at 17, the players were all high-fiving each other.

However, Del noticed that Cade's face had the kind of look he had over the previous years, a look that said he was not as enthusiastic as his teammates. Del hoped that it was just Cade being focused and intense. As he spoke to the boys in the huddle and glanced at each of them while talking, he noticed Cade behaving in the same way he had in huddles in the past—either head down looking at the floor or head up looking out at the crowd. He had no eye contact with Del and he did not look at what Del was drawing on his white board. In mid-sentence, Del jarred Cade back into attention with a firm, "Cade—over here!" Cade looked at Del then at the white board, and he seemed to be focused in on what Del was saying.

As they broke the huddle with all hands in together up high, Del noticed Cade on the outside of the huddle and starting to lean out as if to walk out onto the court. Once again, Del said, "Cade—In here!" Cade leaned back toward the huddle and put his hand up with all the others. As usual, Remington was in the center of the huddle and said, "Team on 3... 1, 2, 3," and the team yelled, "TEAM!"

Bitterroot went on a 7-0 run to start the second quarter. They opened with a corner 3-pointer, and then pounded the ball inside to their two big men on the next two possessions, and the outsized Wolves couldn't stop them. At the other end of the floor, Nick made a nice move to the basket, but couldn't get the layup to fall, and Remington had a good look at an open 3-pointer that rolled around the rim before popping out. Cade turned to Remington and gave him a look of disgust. While he didn't say anything, his facial expression spoke volumes.

Unfortunately, as the quarter went on and Bitterroot's lead extended to 12, Cade's demeanor continued to get worse. He barked at teammates to "work harder," and he glared at them when they didn't pass him the ball. Sacajawea cut into the Bitterroot lead with their press by getting a couple of steals and layups. On a 3-on-1 break, Remington had the ball in the middle with Cade on his right and Billy on his left. Remington leaned toward Cade and looked at him, causing the defender to lean toward Cade, exactly what Remington wanted. As Remington looked at Cade, he fired a right-handed bounce pass off the dribble across his body to Billy that hit him in perfect stride, and Billy easily dropped the ball off the backboard into the net. It was a great pass, and the crowd acknowledged it with "Oohs" and whoops of applause. The lead was now 6, and the Bitterroot coach called a timeout.

Heading to the bench, Cade yelled at Remington, "I was open! Get me the ball!"

Remington responded, "Are you kidding me? That kid stepped your way, Cade. Billy was the one who was wide open. Did you see how easy that layup was for him?"

"Look for me, too," said Cade as he sat down on the bench.

Kevin had been focused on Cade from the moment Remington hit Billy with the pass. The pass had been a thing of beauty, but Kevin knew Cade from years past, and he wanted to see how Cade would respond. He could see Cade was not happy, and he heard the exchange between Remington and Cade as they headed toward the bench. He didn't say anything to Cade, but he watched him in the huddle. Again, Cade was not in the right frame of mind in the huddle. Kevin knew that all eyes and all ears had to be on the coach who was speaking in a huddle, or else things could easily break down once they got back out onto the floor.

Del set up a different press than the one they had been in. It was called "Black." Because they had only been practicing for two-and-a-half weeks, Del did not have all of the offenses and defenses they would have in as the season went on, so they had only put in their "White" press for this first weekend. The Black press had a couple of little twists on what they were doing in White, and all the boys in the game at that time had run it a lot last year. Del drew it up on his whiteboard, reminding each player where to be and where to go. Bitterroot would not be prepared for it.

Kevin wondered if Cade heard anything Del was saying during the time-out. Cade had only glanced at the whiteboard occasionally while Del was drawing and talking, and Kevin doubted Cade was hearing anything that Del was saying. Kevin moved over to Cade, tapped him on the shoulder, and pointed to where Del was explaining the change. However, Del was just finishing up, and Cade missed most of the explanation.

As they broke the huddle, this time with Cade already headed out to the floor, Kevin said to Del, "I don't think Cade heard a word you said in there. He was so pissed that Remington didn't throw him the ball on that break that he was in his own little world during the whole timeout. We need to watch him."

As the referee was getting ready to hand the ball to the Bitterroot player, it was obvious that Kevin was right. The other four players got into their positions that Del had drawn up, but Cade was still over in the position he had been in for the previous press. Del yelled, "Cade, get to the half-line!" Cade

Chapter 8

looked over confused, but he dropped back just as the ball was inbounded. The front of the press did exactly what Del had drawn up, and Nick and Remington forced the Bitterroot player right to where they wanted him to go. However, Cade was lost. He had no idea that they had switched up their press. A Bitterroot player broke right to where Cade should have been and easily caught the pass. Cade scrambled to make up for his mistake, but he was too late. In doing so, he left another area wide open for the next pass. Billy had to make up for Cade's mistake, which left the basket unprotected. The Bitterroot player fired a pass to a wide-open teammate for an easy lay-up.

Del yelled, "Cade! We're in Black, not White!"

Cade looked confused. He yelled back at Del, "What's Black?"

Del immediately turned to his bench, pointed at Tim Nelson and said, "Go for Cade." Tim hopped up and trotted to the scorer's table. Cade saw the exchange as he stood at half court, dropped his head, and started jogging up the court. At the next dead ball, Tim went in for Cade. As they passed one another, Tim said, "Who do you got?"

Cade didn't say a word. He just half-jogged, half-walked to the bench. As coaches and players high-fived him, he barely held his hand out for them to do so. His facial expression said, "I am so pissed right now! How dare you take me out of the game." He walked past the bench, got a drink of water and then sat down at the end of the bench.

Del gave him a minute to gather his thoughts. He knew that when a player was already upset, getting on them or trying to correct or critique them was usually pointless, and it could actually be detrimental. So he gave him his time, coaching the boys on the floor.

Tim gave the team a spark. He made a nice back-door cut, and Remington threaded the needle to find him for a lay-up. He then had the steal that Del had anticipated Cade making on the press a moment ago. A quick pass to Nick and one right back to Tim, and he had another lay-up. Sacajawea was down by four points, and they were set up in their press again. This time a Bitterroot player tried to dribble through the press. Billy and Tim were able to trap him and force a pass. Tim deflected the ball into the hands of Brian Jackson who threw ahead to Remington, who was wide-open at the three-point line. He elevated to shoot, saw Nick cutting hard to the basket, and rifled a bullet to him for an easy lay-up. The crowd went wild, and the boys were fired up.

Del looked down the bench for Cade. Cade was sitting at the far end of the bench, three seats away from his nearest teammate. His teammates were whooping and hollering after Nick's layup had tied the game, but Cade was just sitting there, looking down at the floor. He was lost in his own thoughts, and he seemed upset. Here he was in the first game of the season with his team on a run to tie a game without him on the floor, and he could not bring himself to watch. Del wondered if maybe Cade just didn't have what it takes to be a team player.

Del yelled, "Cade!" and motioned for him to come over to him. He wanted to talk to him for a minute before putting him back in the game. Cade looked at Del with a combination of a glare and an "I don't care" look. As he was about to get up, Cade sighed, as if to show that he really didn't want to get up and walk down toward Del. As he slowly started to stand up, Del yelled back down at him, "No, no. Forget it. If you don't want to play that badly, you can just sit there and pout while your teammates are out there busting their butts and over here cheering their hearts out!" Del turned back toward the court to watch the action.

Cade had a look of disbelief on his face. He didn't know what to do. He had been doing everything right for the first weeks of practice. He worked hard, he was nice to teammates, he had fun with them, laughing and joking afterwards. What more did coach want?

Cade couldn't wrap his mind around what was happening. He knew he was better than everyone else on the team, yet it seemed like Coach Brooks wanted him to be just like everyone else. "I'm the best player on the team. Why would you want your best player to not be the best player? Why doesn't he treat me like the best players are supposed to be treated? He's already picking on me. Why does he hate me so much? He better figure it out and realize that they can't win without me."

As the last minutes of the first half wound down, the Wolves were battling hard. It was back and forth action. Down by three points with twelve seconds left, Coach Brooks called a play. Remington directed his teammates to their spots. The play then began with Brian setting a screen for Remington at the point. Nick was in the right corner. As Remington came off Brian's screen, the man guarding Remington got caught up in the screen. As Remington turned the corner around the screen, he saw the open lane to the basket starting to be closed down by Brian's man. This was a cue to Brian to either roll to the basket or step back to the 3-point line, depending on where his man and Remington's man went. Both men worked to cut Remington's drive off. Nick's man stayed tight with him in the corner, so Nick was not an option.

Out of the corner of his left eye, Remington saw Brian step back to the 3-point line. He was wide open. However, with Brian's man cutting off Remington's drive and his own man on his left hip, it would be a difficult pass. Remington took one more dribble to draw both defenders a little more and to create a better angle for the pass back to Brian. He then jump-stopped on both feet, reverse-pivoted, and fired the pass. Brian caught the ball in his shot pocket, elevated, and let it fly. The clock showed three seconds left as the ball swished through the net. By the time a Bitterroot player got to the ball and got out of bounds to try to throw it in, the buzzer went off. The score was tied 36–36.

Ideas to Consider:

- **How does Cade revert back to his old ways?**
- **What mistake did Cade make that caused Coach Brooks to take him out of the game?**
- **Coach Brooks was going to put Cade back in the game. However, he chose not to. Why did he choose not to put him back in? What was Cade's reaction?**

Chapter 9

The Sacajawea crowd was in a frenzy, and the team was hugging and high-fiving as they headed to the locker room—except for Cade. He walked to the locker room with his head down, avoiding eye contact with anyone. He walked into a loud, excited locker room. He wished he was anywhere but there, but at the same time, he wished he could feel the same way as everyone else felt. He knew he had to change his look and his actions quickly, or he would face more consequences from Coach. He flipped a switch, smiled and started high-fiving guys. He was putting on a show, and he hoped Coach would see it.

Cade struggled with the fact that his team played well without him, and he was worried that Coach might not feel the need to play him as much in the second half. He wanted to play badly, so he figured he better act like he was happy for his teammates. He went around to most of his teammates high-fiving them. He didn't say anything, and while he was actually high-fiving them, there was not much spirit or enthusiasm behind it. He couldn't bring himself to get across the locker room to high-five Remington, though.

Cade felt Remington was starting to challenge him as top dog on the team, and Cade didn't like it. He saw it last year, and he made sure he put Remington in his place. He knew he could keep Remington down because Remington was too nice to ever fight back. He was "Mr. Great Teammate" that everyone liked and liked playing with, so he was an easy target to shoot down when he was taking the spotlight off of Cade. Cade was a bit shocked in the summer when Remington stood his ground and talked back to him in the last tournament. He had never done that before, and Cade hadn't known how to handle it. But since it was the end of the summer schedule, there was never another chance to do something about it.

In practice this year, Cade had changed his tactics with Remington and treated him like a friend instead of an enemy, beginning with his "bury the hatchet" moment the first night of practice. Cade thought that was a smooth move on his part to get Remington to think they were somehow friends. He continued it during the school day when he saw Remington in the halls and cafeteria.

As strange as it sounds, Cade struggled with the fact that the two of them played well together in practice. Cade liked how well Remington set him up so well to score. Cade was a better player when Remington was on the floor. Remington was one of those players who always tried to help his teammates be better. He often passed up good shots when a teammate might have a better one. So Cade liked playing with Remington because Remington made Cade look and play better. However, it was a double-edged sword for Cade because that also helped Remington look and play better, too, and Cade didn't like Remington looking better.

As the players took their seats in the locker room, Coach Brooks started talking. He first talked about what went well in the first half. He highlighted the play of Remington and Nick, as well as the spark that Tim gave them off the bench. Tim had a big smile when he heard that, and Bruce Popovich, a senior guard who was sitting next to Tim, gently elbowed him in the ribs and high-fived him. Del talked about the press, and re-diagrammed the switch that they went to in the second quarter, focusing his attention on Cade as he explained it again. Cade was paying attention this time, and when Del asked, "Everybody understand this now?" Cade nodded his head along with the rest of the guys.

Del then talked about some of the things they struggled with. He made some adjustments to how they would defend the big guys inside. He talked about everyone making sure that when Remington had the ball to make sure that they were all stepping to open areas with their hands ready because he would find them and the ball would be there. "Keep looking for these guys, Rem, but don't forget that you're a good shooter, too. When you're open, knock it down."

Del continued. "Coaches, do you have anything?" Kevin talked about making sure that they were all on the same page, all focused in huddles and on the directions that Del was yelling out to the floor. He was speaking to the team, but he hoped Cade was the one hearing him. Braden said that he thought they could run this team off the floor, but they needed the ball to do that, and the only way they could get the ball was to defend and rebound.

Del then said, "Great points, Coaches. All right, anything you guys have to say about what you're seeing out there?" There was a moment of silence where nobody responded. As a junior, Remington didn't want to step on seniors' toes, especially guys like Cade and Billy, who felt like they were the leaders of the team. But Remington was also one of the most knowledgeable players on the team. As a coach's kid himself, he saw things on the floor that others just didn't. He was the ultimate point guard because of this, always knowing what they were running, what defense the other team was in, and where his teammates should be.

When no one else spoke up, Remington said, "Coach, I think if we can keep putting Brian's man in ball screen actions, he's going to struggle. He's big, but he's slow. With all of our good guards who can handle the ball, Brian can screen for any of us and either roll to the hoop or pop out for a 3 like that last play. We just have to read how our men defend it and then make the right play. And for those not in the screen action, slide to that open spot for the jump shot like Nick did. We should get open lay-ups and jumpers off of that all night."

As Remington spoke, Del was nodding and saying "Yes." When he finished, Del said, "Yeah, that's a great point. We can call play #1 if we want, but when we're in our motion, Brian go screen for the ballhandler. Everyone be ready to play off of that action."

As Del started talking, Cade couldn't believe what he had just heard. "Now Remington thinks he's a coach! Give me a break." While Cade could recognize the point was a good one and made sense, he thought, "Who does he think he is? And it's only the first game. What is he going to be like as the season goes on?"

Cade gathered his thoughts quickly while Del was finishing his point. As soon as Del finished, Cade said, "I think we have to look for each other more. When guys are open, get them the ball. This is a team game, and we all need to be team players."

There was a moment of stunned silence. All of the players sat there wondering, "Is anyone else thinking what I'm thinking? Are you serious, Cade? Of all the people on this team talking about looking for each other, you're the one telling us to look for each other. When have you ever looked for a teammate? When have you ever been a team player?" While they didn't speak their thoughts, they all looked at Coach to see what he would say or do.

Chapter 9

Del realized that though it was just the end of the first half of the very first game of a 20+ game season, he had a major decision to make. In the past, he would have said something like, "Cade's right. We all need to ..." In doing so, Del was trying to validate the point, which was a good one, but also let Cade know he cared about him and valued what he had to contribute. If Cade truly meant what he said, then he truly meant all of us when he said "we." However, Cade would then go out and play his usual selfish way and treat his teammates poorly. Del knew he had to deal with this right now, or this would be a repeat of last year.

"What game were you watching out there, Cade?" said Del. "Because I just saw five guys always looking for each other, especially in the second quarter while you were on the bench. Your teammates do that as well as any team I've ever coached. Everyone in here is a team player, Cade, except for one guy—YOU. How about you start being a team player before you start telling other people to be team players?"

While Cade was stunned that Coach Brooks had dressed him down like that, collectively the players on the team were thinking, "Yes! Finally, Coach said something to him." As good as they felt about that, they all wondered if Cade had heard it, if he cared, if he would change, or if he would take out his anger on all of them and be even worse. Only time would tell.

Del said, "All right, everyone up." The players all hopped up and got in a circle, putting their hands up to where Del already had his up above his head. As usual Cade was on the outside, barely close enough to put his hand up in the air where all the other hands were. Del said, "Cade, let's go. Get your hand in here." Cade snapped out of his funk a bit, reached up, and put his hand on top of the other boys' hands.

Del turned back into the huddle and said, "Boys let's take it to this team. Let's keep running and running and don't stop until their tongues are on the floor and their tails are between their legs!"

The boys all shouted, "Yeah! Let's go!" Remington shouted, "Wolves on three—One, Two, Three," and the boys all shouted, "Wolves!" As they headed out the locker room door, Del considered calling Cade back in, but he thought better of it. He turned to Kevin and said, "Was I too hard on Cade?"

"Nope," said Kevin. "It's exactly what he needed to hear. We can't have that this year. He took full advantage of the leash you gave him last year. You need to make sure that he does it your way this year, not you doing it his way." Del couldn't tell if the shoe was on the other foot, and he was now the recipient of a minor dressing down by a coach. He realized that Kevin was right, though. Those were the kinds of things that made Del glad Kevin was on the staff.

"Do me a favor," said Del. "Will you make sure Cade is all right? I don't want to put him in a tough spot right now having to deal with me."

"Oh sure, let me go into the lion's den," Kevin said sarcastically. "No problem. I've got this." They took three more steps, and then Kevin said, "However, he's going to need to know that you are fine with him, and he's going to need to know that sooner than later. I'm sure that was hard for you to say to him, but I'm even more sure that was harder for him to hear it. Let him know you believe in him, but you also need him to believe in his teammates. His comment in there wasn't about his teammates not looking for each other. It was actually about how they don't look only for him. That makes it look like he doesn't believe in them, that he's the only one who can do this. The more he looks for them, the more they will look for him."

As Kevin headed to bench, Del headed toward Cade, who was shooting jump shots from the corner. He said, "Cade," and nodded for him to come over to him.

Cade stepped off the court after shooting a three and looked Del in the eye without saying anything. "You're starting again this half." Del then said, "I know I was a bit harsh with you in there, Cade, but I can't let you get away with that this year. I don't know if you can see the irony in you, of all people, calling out your teammates for not being team players. If you ever figure out that when you get them the ball and involve them more, they will be turning right back and getting you the ball in even better spots, we're going to have a stellar season, and you're going to become the player you want to be. There isn't a selfish player on this team, Cade. For them, it's not about them. It's about us. They all just want to win and have fun playing together." Del paused to see if what he was saying registered, but he couldn't tell.

"I believe you can be that same kind of guy, Cade. But the guy who we saw in the second quarter and in the locker room and all last year, he has to leave for that new guy to show up. The old Cade can't be on this team if we, and you, are going to have the success we all want. The guy who I think is inside you, the guy who cares about his teammates, that's the guy we need to come out and play for that to happen. Get it?"

"Got it."

"All right. Let's have a great half." As Del walked to the bench, he wondered if Cade truly "got it." He hadn't ever gotten it before. Why would one scolding and a short talk make him get it now? Del thought sarcastically, "Why is it that I like coaching so much when I have to deal with this kind of stuff?" He looked out at Remington, Billy, Brian, Nick, and Tim shooting and laughing with one another and thought, "Oh yeah. That's why."

Ideas to Consider:

- Why does Cade struggle so much with Remington as his teammate?
- What was Cade's comment at halftime that had the entire team in shock? Why did they feel that way?
- How did Coach Brooks respond to Cade's comment? Do you think that was a good response? Why or why not?
- What does Coach Brooks mean when he tells Cade, "The guy who we saw in the second quarter and in the locker room and all last year has to leave for that new guy to show up"?

Chapter 10

The second half started out well for the Wolves. Cade was actually being a great teammate, passing, talking, high-fiving guys, and the team was playing well. They were certainly better when he was on the floor, as his skill level was so strong. The question remained, though, if they were a better "team" when he was on the floor. When he behaved and played the way he did for the first five minutes of the second half, the answer was a resounding "Yes."

Del sent Bruce Popovich into the game for Cade with 1:27 left in the third quarter and the Wolves holding onto a six-point lead. Del wanted to give Cade a breather to make sure he was fresh for the fourth quarter. Three other subs were already out on the court spelling other starters, leaving only Remington on the floor with four subs. However, Del had faith in his "second team," and he knew Remington would make sure they were in the right spots. He also knew Remington could carry the load a bit until the starters got back in.

As Cade saw Bruce Popovich trotting out to the floor, pointing at him, and calling his name, he thought, "Are you kidding me? Again? He's taking me out again? What did I do wrong now?" Cade walked from the far end of the court toward the Sacajawea bench, and the referee had to say to him, "Let's go. Hustle up." Cade started a slight jog to the bench.

When he got there, Del met him on the sideline, extended his arm to high-five him, and said, "Great job, Cade. That's exactly what we need from you. Keep that up."

Cade said, "Then why are you taking me out? What did I do wrong?"

Del was constantly amazed at Cade's lack of self-awareness. Del tried to stay calm. "You didn't do anything wrong, Cade. I took you out because we have a minute left in the third, and we're up by six. I want you to be fresh for the fourth quarter."

Chapter 10

"But what about Remington? He played most of the first half, and I didn't play much at all. And he's still out there."

"Seriously, Cade! You're upset that one of your teammates is playing more minutes than you? What are you, a 7th grader? Remington is coming out next. I wanted to keep a starter on the floor to be with the next four."

"Well, why not me? I sat the whole 2nd quarter. I'm fresher than he is."

Del was starting to see what was going on. It wasn't just that Cade was selfish and not a good teammate. That had been obvious for years. This was more than that. Cade was jealous of Remington. Cade saw Remington as a threat to his status, his position as the "best player," his perception that he somehow had power. Cade struggled with the attention Remington was getting, which in Cade's mind, was taking the spotlight off of Cade.

Del knew he couldn't address this now because, quite honestly, he didn't know exactly what to say that would not create more feelings of jealousy and animosity for Cade towards Remington. He knew he needed them to be good teammates to one another to have any success this year, and he didn't want to jeopardize that, especially in the first game of the year.

"Cade, I want you back out there to start the fourth with the other three starters while Remington is getting his breather. I need you to be out there leading them. But I need you leading them in the best way possible—fresh and as a great teammate. Can you do that?"

Cade felt better knowing that Coach wanted him to be the leader of the other better players. "Yeah, okay. I got it." Cade headed to the bench.

Del sat down next to Kevin and Braden and said, "Did you hear that?"

"Yeah. It's not just his selfishness," said Kevin. "It's Remington." Kevin had seen signs of Cade's jealousy for Remington for a little while, and he wondered when it might rear its head.

"I didn't see that coming," said Del.

"I did," said Kevin. "I had a few kids like Cade before, and they each had a problem with another player on the team stealing their spotlight."

"What do you think I should do? I wanted to tear Cade's head off when I heard him whining about Rem, but I don't want to hurt their relationship even more."

"Yeah, and you also don't want to hurt your relationship with him even more," said Kevin. "You need to be careful with how you handle it, but you will need to deal with it. I've got a couple of ideas, but let's talk after the game. Right now, just keep stressing 'team' with Cade."

The third quarter came to an end, with Bitterroot giving Sacajawea a taste of their own medicine by hitting a three-pointer at the buzzer to cut the lead to two. Del had sent Cade, Nick, Brian, and Billy to the scorer's table as the buzzer sounded to check in for Remington and three of the other subs. He left Bruce Popovich in with the starters.

As the players came trotting off the floor, Cade went up to Remington to tell him he was subbing in for him. He took pleasure in knowing that he got to go in for Remington. When Cade told Remington he was going in for him, Remington said, "Okay. Let's go Cade! You've got this. You had a great third quarter. Keep it up!"

Cade was a bit startled and thought, "Why isn't he upset he's coming out?"

Remington went down to each of the five guys who would be starting the fourth quarter and who were now sitting on the bench, high-fiving them and saying, "Let's go, boys! We got this. Keep this thing going!"

Cade thought, "What do you mean 'we' got this? You aren't going to be in. You're not part of the 'we' who've got this." Cade just couldn't figure Remington out.

During the huddle, Kevin made his way over towards Cade, who as usual was sitting on the end. Kevin just stood by him. Just like the moment Kevin saw Cade start to drift and not pay attention, he tapped Cade on the shoulder and point toward Del who was drawing something up on the whiteboard. Cade immediately turned his attention back to Del. He stayed focused the rest of the timeout, and as the huddle broke, Kevin gently grabbed Cade's elbow and said, "Cade." Cade stopped and kept looking at the floor. "Look at me, Cade." Cade looked up at Kevin. "Your team needs you now. They need you to lead, okay?"

Cade said, "Okay," and started walking out to the floor. However, Kevin grabbed his arm again, this time just a little more forcefully.

"But they need you to lead them for them, Cade, not for you. They need you to be the best team player you can be right now. You can't do this alone,

Chapter 10

and they can't do this without you. Do you understand?"

Cade was a bit taken aback. Coach Nixon had never spoken like this to him before. Cade knew Coach Nixon was a good coach, and Cade liked him, but he had no idea Coach Nixon felt this way about him. Cade felt good, knowing that Coach Nixon felt they couldn't "do this without you."

The part about not being able to do this alone was interesting to Cade, though. Cade knew basketball was a team game, but he also knew he was good enough to beat his man most of the time. He didn't understand why coaches didn't see that and just let him do that. But the way Coach Nixon had just said that made sense. "They can't do this without you." That had always made sense to Cade because he had always felt that he was the best player, and they needed him to succeed. But the "you can't do this alone" made sense, too. "I need them for me to be able to do what I do best, too." That made sense, too.

Cade said, "I got it, Coach," and this time he really meant it.

Ideas to Consider:

- While Cade would be upset about coming out of any game, why was he so upset about coming out at the end of the third quarter?
- What was Remington's reaction when Cade told him he was going in for Remington? Why did his reaction shock Cade?
- What message was Coach Nixon trying to get across to Cade?

Chapter 11

The fourth quarter started out well for the Wolves. Cade was clicking well with the other four players. They were pressing and pushing the ball, and they jumped out to a seven-point lead. Del put Remington back in for Bruce Popovich two minutes into the quarter.

On the first play with Remington back in the game, a Bitterroot guard was dribbling around a screen. Cade was guarding the dribbler, and Remington was guarding the screener. Remington jumped out quickly on Cade's man, while at the same time reaching his right hand out where he thought the ball would come up off the floor. He was able to flick it away. Cade immediately started to take off down the floor. Remington dove for the ball just before it went out of bounds. In one fluid motion while prone and in the air, he grabbed the ball and flung it behind his back towards Cade streaking to the other end of the floor. The ball landed in Cade's hands in stride, and he laid it in the basket.

The Sacajawea crowd went crazy, and as Remington got up off the floor from out of bounds and ran back out to the floor, to get to his place on the press, Cade made a beeline for him while getting to his place on the press. When he got to him, Cade yelled, "Great play!" and high-fived Remington.

On the inbounds pass from Bitterroot, Remington forced the dribbler up the sideline into a trap with Nick. The ballhandler was stuck, but he saw an open man stepping to the middle of the floor. What he didn't see was Cade sneaking up behind him. As the pass was made, Cade stepped right in front of the man and picked it off. He saw Remington ahead of him and fired a bullet pass to him. Remington laid the ball in the basket, pointed at Cade and said, "Nice pass." Cade smiled and pointed back at him. With his team down by 11, the Bitterroot coach called timeout.

While the team was coming to the bench, Del and Kevin looked at each other, and Del said, "If only it were this way all the time, huh?"

Chapter 11

Kevin nodded and said, "No kidding."

For the entire timeout, Del talked about keeping the pressure on and playing with their "pedal to the metal." He never once picked up his whiteboard. He merely talked about playing hard, playing smart, playing together, and burying this team with energy, effort, and team play. Kevin watched Cade for the entire timeout. Cade's eyes never left Del; he was fully engaged. "Maybe he's starting to get it," thought Kevin.

For the next three minutes it was more of the same for Sacajawea, with them pressing and trapping the bigger, slower Bitterroot players. While Bitterroot had some success inside, nothing came easy. It was also obvious they were gassed from having to deal with the speed and pressure of Sacajawea. The lead was extended to twenty-two with just under two minutes left. Del put in the players on the end of his bench because he knew the lead was safe, and Bitterroot's coach did the same.

After the game, the players went through the handshake line and then ran into the locker room with whoops and hollers, high-fiving fans along the way. When Del got into the locker room, he tried to calm the team down a bit. While he wanted them to enjoy these moments, he also knew the value of not getting too high or too low. He said, "Boys, boys. Listen up. That was an awesome start to your season. You faced your share of adversity in a variety of ways. But you persevered through it and came out on top. The key was how well you played together." Del looked at Cade, who was actually looking up at him.

"When we all play together and give of ourselves to one another, there is no limit on what we can accomplish. When we play for ourselves, though, then our limitations become not only evident and obvious, but they also become crippling. Keep playing for each other and watch this thing grow." Del paused for a moment.

"Let's also keep this in mind. Tonight is just night #1. We can't get too caught up in one victory. We have another test tomorrow, and it will be a test of a different kind. Two Medicine will be a whole different kind of team than Bitterroot. Two Medicine is a lot more like us—wide-open, fast, loose, pressing, and pushing. Tonight, we beat a team due to our speed because they couldn't handle it. Tomorrow night we will face a team that can not only handle it, but wants to play that way and does it well. We still want to play our game, but we will have to be smart about knowing when to step on the gas and when to ease off of it."

Del thought about going on about Two Medicine, but he knew that most of what he would say from here on out would go in one ear and out the other. Kids need time and space after games, even big wins. He needed to wrap this up and get out of there. He continued, "But we'll talk more about Two Medicine tomorrow before the game. Tonight, let's enjoy this. I want you to go out there right now and say "Thanks" to your family, friends and fans out there for their support. You have five minutes. Then get back in here and get showered. Then we'll go eat, get to the hotel, and get some rest."

Del called all of them up to huddle up, and as they put their hands into the circle, he noticed Cade right there in the middle of it, a place he normally was not. Del said, "Cade you want to break us down?"

Cade yelled out, "Wolves on three... 1, 2, 3," and they all yelled, "Wolves!" As the huddle broke, the players made their way out the door to go see their families and friends—except for Cade. He headed to his locker and sat down. Del said, "Cade, aren't you going to go out and see your family?"

Cade said, "They're not here. My dad couldn't get away from work, and my mom's out of town." He dropped his head. Del felt bad for him.

"Oh, that's too bad. They missed a good game."

Cade said, "Yeah, I know."

Del then said, "You know, you missed a good game, too, for a while there." Cade looked a little puzzled momentarily, but he then caught Del's meaning. "You spent all last year doing the same things like you did in the second quarter tonight—fighting me and fighting your teammates. That was no fun for any of us. Was that fun for you?"

Cade looked at the floor and didn't say a word. Del continued. "I won't have it this year, Cade. Your teammates won't have it. Wasn't that a whole lot more fun in the second half? Didn't you enjoy that a whole lot more, playing with your teammates in that way instead of just focusing on yourself?"

Cade nodded and smiled. "Yeah. That was a lot of fun."

"Then why do you continue to fight us all on it? Why can't you see that the more you play like that, the more fun you will have and the more success we will all have?"

Cade looked at Del. "I don't know, Coach. I don't know what happens to me. It's like when I step out on that court, I need to be the one. I need to score. I need the glory. I don't know why. Ever since I was little and my dad was coaching me, I felt that way. He always set things up for me to be 'the star.' I was always the best player on my teams, so he always ran everything for me."

Cade paused, starting to realize something that he had not put into words before. "I guess I have always been that way because I always played that way. My dad always talked basketball at home and talked about all the things I needed to do to get my shots. He never talked about my teammates. I guess that just became a big part of who I am as a player. I don't want to blame my dad for it, but maybe that has affected me."

Del asked, "And is that who you want to be?"

Cade looked at Del. Del could see tears starting to build up. "No," he said.

Del said, "Then how can I help? What can I do to help you be the way you want to be?"

Cade looked at the floor. He thought for a moment. "I'm not sure, Coach. I just don't know how to do that, so I'm not sure."

"That's okay, Cade," said Del. "It's going to take some time. But let's talk after we've had a little time away from it and see if there aren't some things I can do to help you with this and if there aren't some things that you can do to help you with this, okay?"

"Okay," said Cade.

Del said, "All right. Why don't you go out there and say, 'Thanks' to some of the fans who showed up and cheered us on? It would mean a lot to them to see you out there, and it would mean even more to your teammates to see you out there with them."

"Good idea, Coach." Cade stood up, wiped his eyes, and started for the door. He stopped, turned around, and said, "Hey, Coach." He paused, then said, "Thanks."

"No problem, Cade. Like I've told you from day one—I believe in you, and I'm here for you... anytime."

Cade nodded, turned, and headed out the door. As Del followed him to go say his own "Thanks" to people, he thought, "This could be a long year." Then he thought, "But it could also be a great year. I hope we can get him on board… for our sake… and for his."

Ideas to Consider:

- How was Cade different in the 4th quarter? What effect did that have on the team and the game?

- What do we learn about Cade from his conversation with Coach Brooks after the game that might be a clue as to why he has behaved the way he has in the past?

- Do you have anything from your past that might lead you to behave in certain ways now? Can you work on those things and change who you are if that would be better for your team?

- What lesson can we all learn from Cade's situation growing up for dealing with our team members?

Chapter 12

The next night, the Wolves played Two Medicine, a school on the Blackfeet Indian Reservation in the northwest portion of the state bordering Canada. It was a good chance for both teams to see how they stacked up against each other and against teams that played similar styles. Indian schools tended to play loose, fast, and up-tempo all the time. It was a fun style of ball to play and just as much fun to watch.

Just like Del figured, the game against Two Medicine brought its share of challenges in a variety of ways. The team faced a very strong opponent who played their style well. Individually, Cade faced his share of challenges where he could have behaved one way or another. To his credit, if he struggled with the teammate part of things, he didn't show it. He was being a good teammate, and the team was rising to the challenges it faced.

True to form, Two Medicine was running and gunning. Sacajawea was, too, but they were not as loose and free. While they liked to push and press, they still focused on getting good shots, shots that came from places within the flow of the offense. Two Medicine, on the other hand, looked as if they had no limits to when and where they would launch a shot from. It seemed as if every player on the team had a green light to shoot it from anywhere.

Their style played havoc with Sacajawea's defense which was not used to opponents shooting those shots. It also opened up offensive rebounding lanes because the Sacajawea players were not ready for shots when they came, and the Two Medicine players knew that at any moment a teammate was firing. Therefore, Two Medicine got a lot of points off of offensive rebounds. Their players were always around the rim, and the ball seemed to find them.

The other way this style can play havoc with an opponent is on their own offense. It is easy to get caught up in this style of play and start trying to play it yourself. All kids want to play this way at some point in their lives, and they all believe they can do it well. However, if it is not how you play normally, and you are in a game with a team that plays this way, you can get sucked into it because it's fun to play this way.

The problem is that when you don't practice this way every day, three things start to happen. First, you don't do the "little" things you normally do. Any discipline that you have worked to make a key to your offense gets easily cast aside. Second, your conditioning level is not prepared for it. You may run and work on your fast breaks in practice, and you may do conditioning after practice, but if you are not used to playing this way for the full thirty-two minutes of the game, by the fourth quarter, your legs and lungs are shot. Usually, this is when teams like Two Medicine take advantage of you because they have no problem with it. Finally, because the first two things happen, you start to turn the ball over. The ball handling and passing that are usually crisp and clean starts to falter. Fatigue starts to get the best of you, and you start to second-guess yourself. Or you never second-guess yourself, but your execution is lacking because you are fatigued and can't make plays the way you normally do in a slower game. This is when the Two Medicines of the world jump all over you and make runs of 6, 8, and 10 points in the blink of an eye.

That is exactly what happened to the Wolves. While they played a similar style to Two Medicine, Two Medicine played at another pace, another level. The Wolves hung with them for a lot longer than most teams. They were clicking, finding each other, and at times scoring easy buckets. That was one of the positives playing against teams like Two Medicine. If you picked and chose your spots, you could be the one that goes on scoring runs. Because Two Medicine played so loose and free, they would take chances that other teams wouldn't. If you had the discipline and the courage to attack them properly, you could get a lot of open layups against them. And the Wolves did just that through the first three quarters.

At the end of the third quarter, Sacajawea was up by two. When they came to the bench, the players seemed upbeat, but Del could tell they were tired. It was early in the season, and they were not used to playing at this pace as much as Two Medicine was. Del had a decision to make—keep pushing and playing this way, or slow things down, take the air out of the ball, and make Two Medicine chase them. He decided to keep playing fast. It was the second game of the year. It was a non-conference game. These were games to test things, try things, and see where a team stood. It was also a game to use as a teaching moment, something to build upon for the conference season that was coming up. "We want to be a running team," Del thought. "Let's see what we're made of and how much work we have to do to become one."

In the huddle Del told the boys, "Great job! You're pushing the action well. They're not used to very many teams hanging with them at their own game. How are you feeling?" Del looked at their faces as most were nodding their heads and saying, "Good." He made a mental note that while their words said, "Good," their faces and body language said, "Tired."

In games like this, you need to rely on your bench a bit more than normal. That was a double-edged sword. While fresh bodies meant fresh legs and lungs, it also meant players not used to being in moments like this against teams like this. Two Medicine always played a lot of bench players, and they all played the same way. On any given night, any player on their team could lead them in scoring because they all played that way and were all used to it.

But for opponents, it could be overwhelming. Del knew he needed his bench guys to step up over the next two minutes in order to have his starters ready to finish off the game. To start the fourth quarter, Del kept Remington on the floor. He was the best-conditioned player on the team. Del debated on whether to give Cade a rest. Cade was also in good shape, although because he didn't give maximum effort in the conditioning, he wasn't in as good a shape as he could be. But Del decided it would be better for him to be playing, so he left him in.

Along with Remington and Cade, Del started Bruce Popovich, Cory Wilson and Mike Visteen. Cory was a tall, lanky, forward. Cory was the tallest player Sacajawea had, standing at 6' 4". He was an up and coming junior who had a nose for the ball, but lacked consistency to his game. Mike was a junior guard who shot the ball well. However, he struggled with his ball handling, and Del worried how he would handle Two Medicine's pressure. For the last two minutes of the third quarter, both Cory and Mike had been in, and they both held their own. Del knew that he would need both of them to grow and develop as the season went on. What better time to start than in an early-season non-conference tournament game that would mean nothing in the standings and everything in kids developing and gaining valuable playing time?

Two Medicine ratcheted up their pressure defense to start the fourth quarter. Mike turned the ball over in the back court and Two Medicine tied the game off the layup that followed. Remington received the ensuing in-bounds pass. He was comfortable with the ball and did not worry about Two Medicine's pressure. He ball-faked and blew past a Two Medicine trap. He was dribbling up the middle of the court when he saw Cade streaking up the right lane. However, he also saw a Two Medicine defender stepping over from behind Cade to step in and steal a pass. The Two Medicine player had been defending Bruce Popovich in the corner behind Cade. Remington saw Bruce positioned behind the three-point line.

Remington looked at Cade as he picked the ball up off the dribble, and like he figured, the Two Medicine defender continued to step towards Cade. With his eyes and body facing Cade, Remington fired a two-handed chest pass right behind the fast-moving Cade to a wide-open Bruce standing in the corner. Bruce caught it and launched a three-pointer. It hit back of the rim, then the front, and then bounced up and over the backboard, out of bounds. Remington yelled ahead to Bruce, "Don't worry about it. Keep shooting. That's a good shot."

Cade turned to Remington and yelled, "No, it's not! Get me the ball. I was wide open."

Remington was a bit startled. Cade had not spoken like this since last night's game. For the first three quarters, he had been the best teammate any of the guys had ever seen him be. Remington quickly shot back, "No you weren't. That kid was coming up quick on you."

Cade said, "Well, I could have taken him. None of these guys can stop me."

Remington headed over to his spot on the press as Cade headed across the court to do the same. Two Medicine entered the ball and quickly advanced it through the press. Cory and Mike looked lost. They got so few repetitions running the press in practice that they were not sure where to be and where to go with each pass. In just four passes, Two Medicine's post man had a lay-up, and they took the lead.

Cory grabbed the ball out of bounds and threw it in to Cade. Cade turned quickly and thought, "I don't need these guys." He swept the ball low across his body and attacked the two players that were coming to trap him.

Chapter 12

He blew past the both of them. However, he was not ready for the next one. As he passed the two who had trapped him, a third defender stepped in his path. Cade used a crossover dribble move, but the defender deftly poked the ball away cleanly, and picked the ball up. He threw a pass ahead to one of the two players in the original trap for another layup. Two Medicine was up by four.

Del called a thirty second timeout. As they were headed to the huddle Cade yelled at his teammates, "I need help out here!"

Remington said calmly, "I thought you said none of those guys can stop you."

Cade didn't have a response, and they were now at the huddle. Del had a decision to make—leave Cory and Mike on the floor and risk them losing confidence against the pressure, or take them out right now and risk them losing confidence for being taken out. If Del took them out, that confidence hit could be worse because they might think Del didn't believe in them. Del decided to leave them in.

Del said, "This is exactly what we knew they would do. They go on runs like this. The key is that a four or six-point run doesn't become a 10- or 12-point run, okay? Relax, but focus. Keep looking to attack, but do so smartly. We can't just dribble through their press." Del looked right at Cade. "That's exactly what they want us to do. We need to pick it apart with ball fakes and diagonal passes. The passing lanes will open up diagonally. Be careful, though, of throwing cross-court horizontal passes. Those kinds of passes lead to steals and layups for them."

Del paused for a second and said, "Boys, we're fine. This is exactly where we want to be. We need to learn how to deal with this because we will face other teams like this during the season. I also wouldn't be surprised if we see these guys again in the state tournament."

Del's words reminded them of their goal—"Get to State!"

Del continued, "Calm down, beat the press, and if you can attack at the end of it, do so. Otherwise, pull it out and run good offense. Let's take the press off for a while and let's just work on our straight half-court man-to-man right now." Cory and Mike looked relieved when they heard that. They could just focus on trying to stop their own men.

Ideas to Consider:

- **How is the Two Medicine team different than the Bitterroot team?**
- **While they play much more like Sacajawea, what problems does playing the way Two Medicine plays pose for Sacajawea?**
- **How does Cade react to Two Medicine starting to build a lead? What effect did that have on the game and on Sacajawea?**

Chapter 13

As they broke the huddle, Del thought about his comment about the state tournament. Del wanted them to be focused on the prize. That's why he wrote it on the whiteboard on day one. He mentioned it now, though, because he also wanted them to know he believed in them and that he truly felt they were going to make it to the state tournament, that it wasn't just words on a board. By the end of the season, he wanted it so ingrained in them that it was just a foregone conclusion for all of them. He knew there was a risk that some of them may take that to mean they didn't have to work as hard to do so, but he wouldn't let them get to that point.

Unfortunately, things continued to go wrong for the Wolves. It was one thing to tell players to "calm down, beat the press, and attack it," but it was a whole different thing to do it, especially against a team like Two Medicine and with players who were not comfortable doing so. Mike had a turnover after the timeout, but Two Medicine missed an open jump shot. Cory got the rebound and threw an outlet pass to Remington. Remington brought the ball up the right side of the floor. Cade was running ahead, and Remington hit him on the right wing.

Remington saw an open lane after his pass, and he cut to the basket. The only defender back was stepping out to guard Cade. Remington was wide open at the three-point line with nobody in front of him on his cut. Cade looked at him, raised up, and launched a three-pointer with the Two Medicine defender jumping up to block his shot. The defender tipped the ball as it left Cade's hands, and it fell behind Cade. The Two Medicine player's momentum carried him right to where the ball landed. He grabbed it, and threw it ahead to a teammate cutting to the basket. Two Medicine was now up by six.

Running back down the floor, Remington said sarcastically, "Nice pass, Cade." One of the basic principles that Del taught his teams was to always thank a teammate for a pass that leads to a score. Cade should have passed the ball to Remington for the easy open layup, but instead forced his own three-pointer.

Cade yelled, "I was open."

Remington responded, "How open could you be when you got your shot blocked?!" Remington broke to the left corner to receive an inbounds pass from Cory. As he turned with the ball, Remington saw Mike ahead of him with no one on him. Remington threw Mike the ball, and Mike turned. There was nobody ahead of him, but he froze. He had that classic "deer in the headlights" look, and he tried to throw the ball to Cade who was cutting to the middle of the floor. However, a Two Medicine player stepped in front of the pass, stole it and went right down the lane for an easy layup. Two Medicine was now up by eight.

Del immediately called timeout and sent Nick, Billy, and Brian to report to the scorer's table. As Mike was headed off the floor, Cade yelled at him, "Come on! Make good passes!"

Mike looked shaken, and Remington immediately went over to him. "Don't worry about him," he said. "You know how he is. You did fine. You'll be all right." But Mike didn't know if that was true. He hoped Del would not put him back in the game.

Del made some adjustments for the new group that was to be on the floor. He felt comfortable that they could handle things. But as the quarter moved on and the pace stayed the same, Del could see that his boys just didn't have the legs, the lungs, or the mindset to stay with Two Medicine the rest of the way. With 1:45 to go, Sacajawea was down by 18. Del emptied his bench, and the starters came off the floor dejected and tired. Cade had a couple of comments for Nick and Remington as they headed to the bench, but they ignored him.

Afterwards in the locker room, Del addressed the team. "Boys, the Tip-Off Tourney is just that—the tip-off to the season. It gives us a chance to play against opponents we won't see in the regular season, and it lets us see where we stand. We faced two good teams this weekend, and we did a lot of good things. We played against two teams with totally different styles. I am so glad we got to play these two teams. Would you have rather we just come over here and played two weak opponents who we crushed and didn't learn a thing from?"

Chapter 13

Del looked around, and most of the boys were shaking their head no. "These two games were about learning who we are and then adjusting to become who we can be. I'm glad we faced Two Medicine today after playing Bitterroot last night. I'm glad we had to face their pressure and the adversity and all that came with it. It's good for us to learn where we stand."

He paused for a moment. "After last night's game you might have thought, 'We're really good.' That's a dangerous thing to think after just one game. That's a dangerous thing to think at any time if you're not careful about it. You walk a fine line with that concept. Yes, it's good to think, 'We're really good,' if you understand why you're really good, what got you to that point. It takes consistent work habits every single day to get to a point where 'We're really good,' is a good thing to be thinking.

"Today, though, we learned that maybe we're not as good as we think. That doesn't mean we're not good. It just means we have a lot of work to do to get to where we want to be. We can play the way Two Medicine plays. But first, we have to get in a whole lot better shape to do so." A lot of players nodded their heads at that. They were exhausted.

"We also have to get a whole lot smarter about how we will play like that. And finally, we have to play a whole lot more together. Too often on both nights we had players trying to do too much on their own." Everyone but Cade was thinking of Cade as Del said that. Del, however, intentionally said "players" because he wanted everyone to understand that any of them and all of them had their moments.

"There is another fine line in this game. The line of 'me' and the line of 'we.' You need both of them to have success in a team game. You need players to be able to play well with their individual skills. It's critical to a team's success. However, you also need all the players with all their different and unique individual skills to blend those skills together, for the good of the team. When we focus on taking our individual skills and playing within the team framework, we maximize our potential."

Del paused for effect. He knew most of the players got that message. He was concerned about one in particular, though, and again, he hoped Cade was hearing it. He continued, "Let me ask you a question."

Del paused, as he waited for all of the boys to look up at him. Once he saw they were all focused on him, he said, "Do you think Two Medicine has kids with strong individual skills?"

63

There were a variety of "Yes" comments. Various players came to mind for different kids as they thought back to the game. Then Del said, "All right, let me ask you a few more. Which one of them was their leader?"

Del paused. "Who took the most shots?"

Del paused again. "Who did we need to stop more than anyone else?"

The boys looked confused. Various names, faces, and numbers were going through all of their heads. Nobody was saying anything. Finally, Billy Thompson said, "Old Chief."

Nick said, "I thought that Davis was really good."

Remington said, "Yeah he's good, but I thought their key guy was Not Afraid. His name was perfect for him, too. That guy played with no fear. He was relentless. You know, actually though, I thought Kipp was their stud."

Remington paused for a split-second as he thought about it. Nobody else said anything, so Remington said, "I don't know, Coach. They were all good. It seemed like every guy just stepped up and played. It seemed like everyone was making an impact, and it seemed like none of them cared who scored, just that they scored. They had a lot of fun out there together."

Del let Remington's words sink in for a few seconds. He said, "That's exactly what I thought. They had fun out there—TOGETHER. If we had to play them again tomorrow, I would not have a scouting report for you guys that was geared to stopping anyone in particular. Because no matter who you try to stop, there is someone else ready to hurt you. That comes first from all of them having solid individual skills. But it also comes from their ability to set aside their own individual skills as the focus of their play, and focus their skills for the good of the team. It's not that they don't have skills and don't want to perform individually. It's that they each maximize what they do best for the good of the team, and they don't care who scores or gets the glory. If each of us does that, we are going to be a really good, or dare I say, even a great team. The key is that the 'if' in that last statement becomes 'when.' WHEN we start doing that, look out Mid-State Conference and look out state of Montana."

Del looked around the room at everyone. Various players were nodding their heads as he finished speaking. "Anyone have anything they'd like to say?"

Chapter 13

"Totally agree, Coach," said Billy Thompson. "All of us have to play together all the time." Other players nodded their approval. Cade was not able to look up at anyone.

Del said, "Thanks, Billy. Anyone else?"

Remington was hesitant. He wanted to speak, but he also didn't want to always be that guy who had to speak up every time they all talked. He felt he was a leader, and he knew his teammates looked up to him that way, so he wasn't uncomfortable speaking up in front of them. It's just that he'd been on teams with players who seemed to think they always had to say something, and often when they did, it didn't come out well. He didn't want to be that guy. Still, he felt compelled to say something. He went ahead anyway. "Coach, everything you said seems spot-on. Last night and tonight, when we played the way you said, it was so much fun, but also, we were so good. I'd say we were unstoppable. But only when we played that way. When we didn't play that way, not only were we stoppable, we weren't all that good."

Remington paused. He knew he and most of his teammates were probably thinking about Cade as the one who this was about. But he didn't want to pile on Cade. He knew they needed Cade to come around and play team ball if they had any chance at achieving their goals. So he was careful not single Cade out. He knew he needed to be considered part of the problem if Cade was going to hear his message. "I'm just as much at fault as anyone. I had my moments where I thought about me more than we out there, both nights."

People looked at him with looks of confusion on their faces. Some were thinking, "When? You never think 'me over we.' You're the most unselfish guy on the team."

Remington figured it might be hard for some to believe that since he rarely did what he just said he did. But he wanted everyone to be thinking about their own play and attitudes. He wanted them to think, "Maybe I do that at times, too." If he could get them all thinking that way, then they would be open to his next statement.

He continued, "I don't know if you felt like you did that at all during these games, but if you did, it's natural. There are times we're all going to do that. But when you're part of a great team and you play with all your friends, it's also just as natural to start playing for each other, to enjoy when everyone else has success, and to stop thinking about 'getting yours' and just think about all of us 'getting ours.' When we are all playing that way, together, this is so much fun, and we are so good, I really believe it. I really think we are unstoppable."

Remington stopped, and leaned back. Nick, who was sitting next to him, fist-bumped him and whispered, "Nice job." Remington felt good and was glad that he had spoken up.

Del said, "Those are great points, Rem. Anyone else? Nobody said anything. "Coaches?" Kevin and Braden both shook their heads no. This was a good place to end it.

Del said, "All right, once again, go out and say 'Thanks to your family, friends, and fans. Be back in here in five minutes to shower, so we can get home at a decent time."

Ideas to Consider:

- **What is the fine line that Coach Brooks is talking about with regards to thinking that you're good? What about the fine line he mentions regarding "we and me"?**
- **What point was he trying to make about Two Medicine players that he hoped might get into his own players' heads?**
- **According to most anyone on the team, Remington is their most unselfish player. Why does he say, "I'm just as much at fault as anyone. I had my moments where I thought about me more than we out there, both nights."? What is his goal in saying this?**

Chapter 14

The Wolves made their way through the season in much the same fashion that the first two games went. Most of the time, they played well together and had great success doing so. While Cade seemed bought in at times, he still had numerous moments throughout the season where he reverted back to the "old Cade." His teammates grew tired of him being selfish in those moments when he did so, but they never said anything about it.

Jenny Jones was still Remington's sounding board. She was always there for him, ready to let him vent or celebrate, depending on how things were going. She knew that no matter what was going on in life, when she and Remington were together, he was going to be talking about basketball. She didn't mind. She liked basketball just fine. What she really liked about basketball, though, was watching Remington play.

She wasn't alone in feeling that way. Remington was one of those players that everyone loved watching. He had a combination of incredible skill, unselfishness, and joy that he exuded out on the court, and it was infectious to anyone who watched. People couldn't get enough of seeing him. And while they came for the ballhandling, passing, and scoring, they fell in love with the smiling and exuberance they saw from him.

While Jenny continued to love watching Remington play basketball for all the reasons everyone else did, she also loved watching him play because she was watching him. As her feelings for him continued to change as they got older, she was attracted to him more. Watching him play basketball was just another way to see him. Since he was always playing basketball, she knew that if she wanted to see him, she would be watching him play basketball.

She also knew that when they were together, she would be hearing a lot about basketball. It's what he talked about all of the time. But she didn't mind. She was someone who was not so connected to the team, like Nick and Tim. She knew that Remington could say things to her that he wouldn't say to them, and he needed that. She liked being there for him. While she was hoping that someday she could be something even more, for now this would have to do, and she was okay with that.

With less than two weeks left in the season, Remington and Jenny were sitting in the cafeteria talking over lunch. He was telling her about how at times Cade was being a great teammate, but how at others he just reverted back to his old self. Remington said he wished Cade would just give himself over to the team completely for the rest of the year. "He just doesn't seem to get it, though. We've tried to tell him that when he plays with us instead of around us, we're a better team, and he's a better player. He nods his head and says all the right things, but then he goes out on the court and still acts like a selfish jerk. It's not all the time, but it's often enough and bad enough that it's affecting us."

Jenny said, "Does Coach Brooks say anything to him?"

"Yeah," said Remington. "He says stuff all the time. But he never really does anything about it. His actions don't follow his words. And now, this late in the season, I don't think he can do much to change things."

Jenny looked at Remington with a sideways glance and asked, "Are you talking about Cade or about Coach Brooks?"

"Good point," said Remington. "I was talking about Coach, but I guess it's the same for both of them. The sad thing is that we have a great chance to be conference champs if we can beat Gallatin this weekend, but if Cade doesn't play with us and Coach doesn't do something about it, who knows what will happen?"

Jenny said, "You know, last year Amanda Hopkins was that way with us out on the soccer field. No matter what we did, she would yell at us, 'Get me the ball on my feet!' She was a good scorer and all, but if things weren't perfectly set up for her, she wasn't happy, and she let everyone know about it."

Remington nodded his head and said, "I remember. She was good, but she drove me nuts, how she would stand up in the front line waiting for you guys to do all the work and get her the ball. And no matter where you put it, I could hear her yelling that it wasn't good enough." He paused as Jenny nodded her head, and then he said, "I remember thinking, 'God, she's a female Cade!' and I kind of laughed. But as I sit here now, I realize that there wasn't anything funny about it. You were going through a lot of the same things I go through with Cade."

"Yep," Jenny responded. "We're just kindred spirits," she said laughing. "Just not the kind of reason I want to be a kindred spirit with you... or anyone else for that matter."

As they both laughed, who should walk up to their table but Cade. He smiled and said, "What are you two love birds laughing about?"

Jenny and Remington both started to blush as they looked up at Cade. They didn't know what to say for two reasons. One, they had been talking about him and didn't know how to respond. Two, he called them love birds. Why did he do that?

"Oh, it's nothing," said Remington. "Jenny was just telling me a story about soccer last year."

Cade said, "Oh, really? What was it? What happened that was so funny?"

Jenny said, "It wasn't anything, Cade. You wouldn't get it." She stammered a bit and said, "I mean, you probably wouldn't think it was all that funny."

"Try me," said Cade.

As Jenny started to struggle to figure out what to say, the bell rang. "Oh, well, gotta' get to class. Can't be late or Ms. Gregory will give me a detention." She got up from the table quickly, grabbed her lunch tray, and as she headed to the window where the lunch ladies were waiting for everyone's dishes, she said, "See you guys."

They both said, "See you Jenny."

Cade turned to Remington and asked, "What was so funny? What happened?"

Remington said, "Oh, it's not actually that funny. And it was kind of personal and a little embarrassing for her, so I don't think I should tell you."

"Oh, I see," said Cade, smiling. "Protecting your little lady, huh? Okay. But I'll find out some way, you can bet on it."

Remington said, "Yeah, I bet you will, Cade. Well, I gotta' get to English. I'll see you at practice."

"All right, see ya' Rem."

As Remington walked away from Cade, he couldn't get what he called them out of his mind—"love birds." And then calling Jenny his "little lady." What was that all about? Did people really think that about them? Did they think they were together in that way? Why? They had always been good friends, and everyone knew that. Why would people all of a sudden think there was more to their relationship than that?

"We've never done anything to show anything like that, have we?" he thought. "Gosh, do we look like we're together like that? What are we doing that makes people think that?"

Then he had a different thought that sent a shiver down his spine. "Oh my God, does Jenny know that I think about her like that? Oh no. What did I do? She doesn't like me like that, does she? I mean it would be cool and everything, but I don't think she thinks of me like that. Does she? What should I do? Should I ask her? No, I couldn't do that. What if she doesn't think that way at all, and I start asking her? Then she'll know that I like her that way."

He didn't realize it because he was so lost in his thoughts walking down the hall, but Nick Bertucci was standing right in front of him. "Dude, what the heck are you doing?" asked Nick. "Where is your mind? You almost ran right into me."

Remington was a bit startled as he realized it was Nick. Nick started walking with Remington as Remington said, "Uh, sorry. I got this assignment due in English, and I was just kind of going through it in my mind 'cause I'm not sure if I did it right."

"Oh yeah, right, Rem," said Nick. "Like you ever have a problem with any assignment. What has your GPA dropped to now—3.96 or something like that? Yeah, I'm sure you didn't do your English assignment right. Quit worrying about it and get focused on what's really important—beating Gallatin on Friday!"

Remington was glad that Nick moved the conversation to that, and he said, "Absolutely! Can't wait to take it to them. But we have to have good practices the next couple of nights."

Nick said, "Yeah, I know that, and you know that. But tell that to Cade. I don't like how he has started going back to the old Cade more lately.

Chapter 14

We need him to play the right way this weekend. But he needs to practice that way first."

"No doubt," said Remington. "I hope Coach says something to him. No matter what we tell him, it seems like it doesn't matter. In fact, he's starting to snap back at us."

"Starting?!" said Nick. "When did he ever stop?"

"Well, at the beginning of the season, he was better."

Nick said, "Yeah, for like a week. For all his talk on the first night, Coach sure hasn't done much about it." Remington nodded and Nick said, "We just gotta' all continue to play together and fight through it. If Cade wants to join in, great, but if not, oh well. We don't need him."

Remington said, "Yeah, I get that you feel that way, and I want to feel that way, too. But the truth is that we do need him. He's really good. We need him to be the player he is, while at the same time being a good teammate. If we can get him to do that, we've got a conference championship banner to put up in our gym."

"I hope you're right, Rem," said Nick. "But like I said about Cade at the beginning of the year—I'll believe it when I see it."

Remington turned to go down the hall to his English class, "All right, Nick, I'll see you at practice."

"Later, Dude," said Nick.

Ideas to Consider:

- **What is Remington's problem with the way Coach Brooks has dealt with Cade during the season?**
- **How is Cade different to Remington in school than he is in basketball? Why do you think that is?**
- **What did Cade say that has Remington worried that people may be noticing about him? How can things like this outside of athletics affect athletes? What can you do to not let something like that affect you in a negative way?**

Chapter 15

Heading into the final two regular season games, the Wolves were 12–4 overall and 5–1 in conference. Their one conference loss was a close one to their archrivals, Gallatin. The Wolves felt like they let that game slip away late. While Gallatin was a good team and battling with the Wolves for first place in the conference, they were by no means filled with superior talent. They had just played well together in that first game, and the Wolves did not, especially late. The Wolves were looking forward to getting them back at home. If they could win this game, they would be tied with Gallatin for the conference championship with one game left.

Cade was having a great season statistically. He led the team in scoring at just over 16 points per game, followed by Remington at 13.5 points per game. But Remington was also leading the team and state in assists at just over 6 per game. Cade was glad that Remington led the team in assists because Cade was the recipient of a lot of those passes. But Cade did not like that Remington was so close to him in scoring.

Cade also didn't like that he was only averaging 16 points per game. He wanted to be up around 20 points per game. That's where all the great ones were. The leading scorer in the state was Josiah Old Bull from Longbow, a school on the Crow Reservation in the southeastern part of the state. He was averaging 21.3 points per game. Then there were two kids in the 20 points per game range and two around 19 points per game, and two at just over 17 points per game. Cade was eighth in the state in scoring. He needed to get higher up that list.

The problem was that all of this emphasis on "team" meant everyone was watching to make sure Cade was playing team ball. He actually liked how much fun he was having playing with his teammates that way, but he didn't like what it did to his scoring average. While he wasn't in the top twenty in the state in assists, he was in the top ten in the conference, aver-

Chapter 15

aging 2.5 per game, which was more assists than he had ever averaged before.

But Cade didn't play the game to get assists. He played to score. He knew that was what would get college coaches interested in him. After one month, he had one college who had shown interest in him, Rocky Mountain College in Billings. They were an NAIA school not an NCAA DI school. Also, they were interested in Remington. Cade couldn't imagine going to the same school as Remington. He'd had to share the spotlight with Remington so far this year. There was no way Cade wanted to do that in college, too.

The rematch with Gallatin was the second-to-last game of the season. It was senior night for the Wolves. For the seniors, Cade, Billy, Bruce Popovich, and Alex Peters, it would be an emotional night. Cade and Billy had been two of the best players all season, and they wanted to showcase their skills for the last time in their home gym. Bruce had seen his minutes dwindle as the season went on as Brian's, Tim's, and Mike's minutes went up. Alex Peters had fought an injury he sustained during the football season that just wouldn't heal, and he was starting to get a few more minutes late in the season, but he was just not the same player he had been as a junior. He and Bruce really wanted to contribute in a big way if they could.

The entire game was a see-saw affair. Neither team led by more than 8 points through the first 3 & ½ quarters. The Wolves were playing well together, and they had a string of eight straight points in the middle of the fourth quarter that put them up by six with just over 4:00 left in that game. As always in games with Gallatin, there was a big crowd on hand, so it was a great high school basketball atmosphere. There were a few college scouts in attendance, even one from the University of Montana, a DI school from the western side of the state.

Because of it being senior night with a large crowd, as well as the scouts being there, Cade felt he needed to distinguish himself. Along with everyone else on the team, he had been playing well on both ends of the floor. He played better defense than usual, and he was finding open teammates for scores. He had 5 assists up to that point, the most he had in any game. However, he had only scored eight points up to that time. Eight points was not going to cut it for college scouts. He decided that he had to take over and do something special.

73

For the last four minutes of the game, whenever Cade got the ball, he did one of two things—whether he was open or not, he would shoot a 3-pointer or drive to the basket and shoot. He only threw three passes in that entire four-minute span, two of which were inbounds passes on out-of-bounds plays. Cade took eight shots in that time, but he only scored twice—a three-pointer and a free throw when he got fouled on a drive. Everything else was a missed shot, which gave Gallatin fast break opportunities. Because Cade took his shots so early in each possession, Gallatin had plenty of time to come back.

With two minutes left in the game, Gallatin took back the lead. While Del tried to keep everyone calm and tried to get Cade to play within the team framework again, Cade panicked. He realized that he was not scoring and that Gallatin was scoring because of that. Instead of playing team ball, however, he pressed even more and decided he needed to make up for his mistakes. His shot selection got worse, and when the game was over, Gallatin had won by six. There would be no conference championship banner hanging in the Sacajawea gym this year.

Walking off the floor, Cade actually felt bad that he had let his team down that way. However, even more so, he felt bad that he finished with only 12 points. If he had just shot more throughout the game, he could have scored more. That's what he needed to do. That's what those college scouts needed to see. That team stuff was good enough for guys like Remington and Billy and Nick. But Cade felt that he was the best player on the team, and the best player needed to score. The only way to do that was to shoot.

As he sat down on a locker room bench off away from the team, he knew he was going to hear about it again from Coach Brooks. But Cade could only think, "Why doesn't he see what I'm capable of? Why doesn't he want me to shoot more? I'm the best shooter. I should get more shots than anyone else. I should be taking games over. Why isn't he running plays for me?"

Del started. "Well, we let one slip away from us there, boys. We had them down, we were playing well, but then we started playing too much one-on-one and not enough team ball."

Upon hearing that, every player but one was thinking, "Sorry, Coach, but you're wrong. We didn't start playing too much one-on-one; Cade did. Why don't you say something to him? Why are you always blaming all of us when it's Cade that does it?"

Chapter 15

Del continued. "We've said it all year long, and it's been proven out all year long. We're really good when we play together. We are one of the best teams in the state when we play together. But when we don't, we're extremely average."

Del didn't know it, but with each sentence, he was losing his team. This had been happening all season long when Cade would play that way. The more Del spoke about how "we" were playing selfishly, the more upset they got with him.

Del looked around the room. He couldn't tell if they were hearing a word he was saying. He figured Cade wasn't hearing anything because by this point in the season, he didn't think Cade had heard anything that had been said all season. The season had begun with such promise for Cade to become a team player, but it appeared the message had not gotten through to Cade. "Why can't I bring myself to address him?" Del thought. "Why do I keep saying this is a 'we' thing, when we all know this is a Cade thing?"

Del didn't want to give himself the answer to that because he knew he didn't like it. He knew it was because he was afraid of the confrontation that it might create. He knew that Cade could blow up at any time. Del didn't want to create a scene in front of everyone, and he didn't want to deal with Cade alone about it. So he did nothing each week and hoped that Cade would figure it out and the problem would go away. So far, neither of those two things had happened.

"Fortunately," Del thought over a matter of a split-seconds, "these are all good kids, and they're okay with me focusing on the team and not Cade. They get it. They understand it's a team game, and every one of us has to play as a team. Every one of them has had moments this year where they played individually. Thank God they all are willing to take their share of the blame. All except Cade, that is. I guess I need to address him at some point."

Del regrouped himself and kept speaking. "Boys, I said it our first night together, and I'll say it again. We have a chance at a very special season. And so far, for the most part, it's been just that. But the rest of the way is only going to get tougher. We need to be playing our best ball come tournament time. Our best ball is when we play together. We need to be buttoned up and on the same page then. That's in two weeks. Let's make sure we all get ourselves re-committed to one another and to playing for one another. Get it?"

There was a collective, but not very enthusiastic, "Got it" from everyone. Remington wanted so badly to say something to or about Cade, but he held his tongue. Nick, however, had been sitting there fuming the entire time that Del was speaking. Cade had said all that stuff that first night at practice about being different this year, yet here he was again being the same old Cade. Nick couldn't hold it in any longer.

"NO! No, Coach, I don't 'got it'! How can you continue to blame all of us?

Del was a bit taken aback, and he started to respond with a sharp "Nick!"

But Nick just continued, "No, Coach. I'm sorry but I can't take it anymore. I just have to say this. How can you continue to say it's all of us? It's one guy, Coach. It's Cade." Nick turned towards Cade as Cade looked up at him with a startled look on his face. "Cade, what the hell is your problem?"

Before Nick could continue, Cade said, "Shut up, Nick!"

But before Cade could say another word, Nick continued forcefully. "No, Cade, I won't shut up! Everyone else has shut up all season long, even the coaches. Nobody wants to say to you what needs to be said to you because 'everyone's afraid of Cade.'" Nick said it in a mocking kind of tone while making air quotes with his fingers as he said it.

"Well, I'm not. I'm sick of it, Cade! Why can't you play with us? Why do you always have to be 'The Man'? Jesus, you act like you don't want anyone else out there with you, like you can just do it yourself. Well, you can't Cade! This is a team game. You need us, but you refuse to believe that. And as much as I hate to admit it, we need you, too. You're really good. But you've got your head so far up your ass, you don't even realize how much you're hurting us, so much so that you're hurting yourself. It's almost comical when you think of it. You want to be all about you, so you look better than everyone else. Every time you play with us, you look great, but every time you play for yourself you look like a selfish pig. You're slitting your own throat, and you don't even realize it."

Nick was so upset that he had tears in his eyes. "When are you going to figure it out, Cade? Or will you ever figure it out? We need you. But we need you to need us. When that happens, this will be awesome. You'll be awesome. But if you don't change, this doesn't change, and we just go back to being average. Figure it out, Cade! We're all sick of it. We're sick of playing

Chapter 15

with you when you play like that. Figure it out or get the hell out of the way!"

Cade wanted so badly to go over and punch Nick right in the mouth. "How dare he talk to me that way! Who does he think he is?" But Cade didn't move, and he didn't say another word.

Del was so stunned by what just happened that he didn't know what to say. Part of him was upset with Nick for challenging him that way. He had never had a player challenge him like that before. Well, Cade had challenged him, but in a different way. However, everything Nick said was true. Del hadn't handled Cade the way he needed to be handled. Del hadn't held Cade accountable. Nick had, in essence, just called Del out in front of everyone, yet Nick was right.

Del struggled with what he should say. He didn't want to lose his team, but he realized that if others felt the same way as Nick, maybe he had already lost them. He stood before them gathering his thoughts.

The locker room was silent for a moment before Del said, "Nick, you're right." He sighed, then said, "Everything you said is right. I'm not only talking about what you said about Cade. Cade, I'll get to you in a second." Cade looked at him. He was so upset and confused that he didn't know how to react. He sat there fuming inside.

Del continued. "You're right about me, Nick. I have let you guys down. I have not addressed the bigger issue. I kept trying to spread the blame around to all of you when we didn't succeed. In doing so, I was absolving the one player, Cade, and the one coach, me, of what each of us was doing that was truly the problem."

Del turned his attention to Cade. He tried to speak calmly. "Cade, he's right. As much as I've said that we need to play like a team, these guys do play like a team all the time. There isn't a selfish player in this room except for you. I have tried to get you to change for three years, but you have refused to do so. Sure, you change for a little while, but then whenever things get a little difficult or the pressure rises, you just go right back to being you. I have talked with you about this in private before, so it's not like this is news to you."

He looked at Nick and the other boys as he said this because he wanted to make sure they knew he had tried to do so before. He continued, "But obviously that hasn't worked. So I'm saying it to you now in front of your teammates."

Del took a deep breath. "I know I should have done this a whole lot sooner in the season, and I hope it's not too late, but we both need to change right now. I need to change and start holding you accountable to all I say that I will hold you accountable to. I need to lead this team properly. And you need to change and start playing team ball 100% of the time. You need to, as Nick said, 'Figure it out or get out of the way.' Otherwise, I will make a different change, and we will move on without you."

Cade couldn't believe what he was hearing. "They aren't moving on anywhere without me. They'll lose out in two at Divisionals without me."

Del was already many steps ahead of him. "We might lose out in two games at Divisionals, but we'll lose out on our terms, not on yours. But you know what? We might lose out in two with you anyway, since when you play selfishly the way you do, anyone can beat us." He paused for a moment and then continued as he turned toward the rest of the team. "And you know what else? We also might not lose out at Divisionals without Cade. We know we're good enough and we've grown enough throughout this season, that I like our chances." He turned back to Cade. "With or without you, Cade."

The boys couldn't believe what they were hearing. Coach was finally saying what needed to be said. Del turned back to all of them. "Boys, I owe all of you an apology. Nick, you're absolutely right. I have not handled this the right way. I kept saying you all were to blame when you weren't. I was afraid to confront Cade because I didn't want to have to deal with what that might bring. But this was so much more important than my feelings and Cade's feelings. This was about our team. This was about us, and I let us down. I am so sorry. I hope you can forgive me, and we can all move forward from this."

They all sat looking up at Del, not knowing what to say or do. Cade just dropped his head. He was crying, but he didn't want anyone to see him. He hated Coach, hated his teammates, hated basketball. He wanted to be so far from there right now. He felt stuck. As Del wrapped up his comments to the team, Cade didn't hear anything he said.

Del said, "All right. It's been a tough night. I am committed to changing and being better for all of you. I hope all of us...," but he stopped. "There I go again. I know all of you are committed to that already, and yet there I was going to include all of you in that, too. Sorry."

Chapter 15

He turned toward Cade. "Cade." Cade slowly raised his head to look at Del. Del could see Cade's eyes were red. "Cade, I hope you're committed to changing with me and being better for all of us, too." Cade hadn't really heard anything Coach had said prior to that, but he nodded his head "Yes," even though he didn't totally agree with it.

"Everybody up here." They all stood and came together in a circle. Cade was slow to get up, but he did so and made his way to the huddle. When all the hands were together above everyone's head, Del said, "Together on three... 1, 2, 3," and they all quietly said, "Together."

After they broke the huddle, Del stepped to the coaches' office door and said, "Cade, Nick. Come here a minute." Both players looked at each other, looked at Coach, and slowly walked to the office.

Del shut the door and said, "Cade, I'm sure that was tough on you." Cade looked straight into Del's eyes trying to show no emotion. "Sorry you had to go through that, but you needed to hear that. I have been trying to tell you that for three years, but it obviously still hasn't sunk in. Maybe hearing that from a teammate, it might." Again, there was no reaction from Cade.

Del turned his attention to Nick. "Thanks for having the courage to speak up that way, Nick. I needed to hear that. I needed to be called out on that. Nobody else did what needed to be done, but you did. I appreciate you having the guts to call me out. I also appreciate you having the guts to say what you did to Cade. I know you don't hate Cade or anything like that. You just want him to play with you guys and be a good teammate." Nick nodded. "I'm glad you said what you said." He turned toward Cade. "I only hope you are, too, Cade."

Cade didn't know what to say. All kinds of thoughts raced through his head. Should he speak the truth or just lie and act like he was fine? As he opened his mouth, he didn't know what he would say or which way he would go with it. "I don't know what to say, Coach. Do you want me to say I liked hearing all that? Do you want me to say I'm happy hearing all that and finding out my teammates hate playing with me? Sorry, but that's not true."

He paused and Del started to speak, but Cade put up his hand and cut him off. "Let me finish, Coach. But if you want me to say that I get it, I do." He turned towards Nick. "I want to kick your ass so badly right now for how you talked to me in there. But I also know how hard that was for you to do, and I know everyone else in there feels that way, but none of them had the guts to say anything. But you did. So as pissed as I am, I also get it, and I guess I'm also glad you did it. I can't promise you anything, cuz I don't know how I'll be or how I'll react in the future. I want to be better. I really do. I just don't know if when push comes to shove, I will be. But I'm glad you did that 'cuz I realize now that I needed to hear that."

"Then you aren't going to kick my ass?" said Nick somewhat hesitantly and somewhat jokingly.

"Not tonight, at least," said Cade with a smile.

"You guys all right, then?" asked Del.

Cade looked at Nick, stuck out his fist, and said, "We cool," and they fist-bumped each other.

Del said, "All right. See you Monday."

Ideas to Consider:

- **What does Cade do during the Gallatin game that leads to them losing?**
- **How does Coach Brooks address it afterwards in the locker room?**
- **What does Nick Bertucci do that nobody else has ever done? Why did he do that? Was he justified in doing so?**
- **Why is it so difficult for Coach Brooks to do what he knows he should do with regards to Cade?**
- **What would you do if you were coaching or playing on Cade's team? How would you have handled things with him?**

Chapter 16

At Monday's practice, after the initial awkwardness of getting back together after the locker room Friday night, there was a whole different feel to things. Cade was like a different player. Everything was about everyone else and very little about himself. He was loose and joking with guys. He passed up shots he would normally take to find open teammates, and he would high-five them on their scores. He was especially friendly with Nick and Remington.

At a water break, Remington quietly said to Nick, "Why didn't you speak up earlier in the season? He's a whole different cat right now."

Nick was guarded. "Remember what he said to you the first night of practice? 'We cool' and then he was all nice to you for a while. Then remember how long that lasted? That's exactly what he said to me in the coaches' office the other night. Let's just see what happens."

"Leave it to Nick to never be optimistic," thought Remington. Remington and Nick were close friends. Remington was always upbeat and positive, always saw the good in things. Nick was more negative. He saw it as just being more realistic. There were times that Remington wished he were more like Nick in that respect. Then he would see how often it seemed like Nick wasn't having fun or didn't see things as positive that truly were positive, and he would think, "No, I'd rather see the positive side of things. It makes me enjoy life more."

But this time, he had to agree with Nick. Remington had been burned by Cade before, and he knew it could easily happen again. But at that practice and for the rest of the week, it didn't. Cade was a joy to be around, and everyone was having more fun with "the new Cade."

Their final regular season game was an away game against the Windwalker Golden Eagles. Windwalker was having a bit of a down season, and with the result of the Gallatin game still stinging, the Wolves needed a team like Windwalker to turn things around and get ready for the Divisional Tournament the following week. While it had been a good week of practice for everybody, including Cade, the real test of whether Cade had gotten the message about being a team player would come in a game.

Cade passed that test with flying colors. He had 14 points, 4 assists, 5 rebounds, and 2 steals—an overall great game. Remington led the team in scoring with 21 points, but he also dished out 7 assists and had 4 rebounds and 2 steals. It was one of the best games anyone had all season. It was also the kind of game that Cade could have been so jealous of that he would be mad about it. But if he was, he didn't show it.

There was one moment in the game when the old Cade appeared for just a moment. Remington had hit a three-pointer, scored on a beautiful drive to the basket, and hit another three-pointer on three straight possessions. The last basket was Remington's 19th point, and there were still 5:00 left to play, with Sacajawea up by seven. On the way back down the floor, Cade yelled to him, "Pass the ball, man!"

Del didn't hear it, but Remington and Nick both did. Remington was in a nice groove, but with Cade starting back into being the old Cade, he was a bit rankled. "Crap," thought Remington. "Here we go again."

Cade then came over to him on the next dead ball and said, "Sorry, man. Old habits die hard. Keep shooting. You're hot."

Remington felt relieved. However, he also worried that maybe he looked like a ball hog. The rest of the game he either passed the ball immediately or drove it and kicked it to a teammate. Usually, the recipient of the pass was Cade. Remington had open looks, but he wouldn't shoot. Cade was in his head, even with his "Sorry" comment. Remington's final points came on two free throws, when he was fouled on a drive when he was actually setting up a pass to Cade. Cade looked upset when the call was made, as he was open for a three-pointer.

The Wolves won by 13, and everyone seemed happy in the locker room. Del's post-game talk was about how the way they played that game is the way they are going to have to play to win at the Divisional Tournament and get to state. The feeling in that locker room was extremely different from the feeling in the locker room the week before. However, as Remington sat there half-listening to coach, he couldn't shake what he was feeling. He

Chapter 16

had just had his best game ever, but he couldn't get Cade's comment about passing out of his mind. He wondered if other teammates thought he should pass more, too.

After showering and getting dressed, Nick, Tim, and Remington were the last players walking out to the bus. Nick turned to Remington and said, "Jeez, for a guy who just had the greatest game of his life, you sure are quiet. What's up?"

Remington said, "I don't know." He continued for a few more steps and then said, "Did you hear when Cade yelled at me in the fourth quarter?"

Nick said, "Yeah, why? Did he yell at you another time, too?"

"No. That was it." He paused. "But he got me wondering. Do you think I was being a ball-hog? Was I shooting it too much?"

Nick and Tim both started laughing. "Are you kidding? You? Shoot it too much? Dude, you need to shoot it more! You're one of the best shooters on the team, but you don't shoot nearly enough. Is that why you didn't shoot in the last few minutes?"

Remington wondered if anyone had noticed. "Kind of. I mean, other guys were open, so I was finding them, but yeah, it was in the back of my mind."

"Well, you need to get it out of your mind," said Nick. "You need to shoot, and you need to shoot more." Nick paused. He then said, "You know all that stuff I said to Cade in the locker room the other night, about being selfish and him needing to play more team ball?"

"Yeah," said Remington.

"Well, the opposite is true for you. There are times you need to get more selfish. You being so unselfish hurts us at times. What if it was close and we needed you to knock down open shots there in the last few minutes? Would you have taken them?"

"I don't know. I think so, but I'm not sure."

Nick made a buzzer sound like you hear on game shows and said, "Wrong answer! You need to shoot it. Just like we need Cade to be more unselfish and pass the ball, we need you to be more selfish and shoot it more. I know that ain't in your nature, but you need it to be at times."

Nick stopped Remington, and Tim stopped alongside them. "Hey, I know it's not you to be selfish, and quite honestly, nobody wants you to actually be selfish and start jacking up shots all over the place. But I am saying that your overly unselfish play is your way of being selfish."

"What the heck are you talking about?" Tim asked Nick.

Remington said, "No, Tim, I actually get it."

"Do you?" asked Nick. "Because if you really do, I wouldn't have to say anything. You don't realize it, but you're just like Cade, but just the complete opposite version of him."

Tim said, "Okay, now I'm totally confused."

Nick continued. "Cade is selfish by being, well, selfish. He just wants shots. He wants to be the man. He wants all the glory. Remington is selfish by being unselfish."

Tim said, "Yeah, see that's where I don't get you. How can he be selfish by being unselfish?"

Nick looked at Remington with a look that said, "Do you want to tell him or should I?"

Remington looked at Nick and then at Tim. He finished Nick's idea. "Because since I'm being so unselfish and not looking to score even when we need me to score, I'm being selfish. I'm thinking only of my feelings and only of me wanting to please everybody and have everybody like me and not thinking of what my team needs from me for us to be successful."

"Bingo!" said Nick. "I'd say pull your head out of your ass and start playing the way we need you to, but quite honestly, I don't think it's your head up there. I think it's Cade's head up there. He's got you messed up. You need to shake him, man, cuz if you don't, you're going to lose your confidence just like last year, and we can't have that at Divisionals."

Remington knew Nick was right because the last four minutes of the game, that's exactly what happened. He had been in a great groove. The basket looked like giant dumpster he was shooting into. He felt like he could blow past anyone who guarded him and get to the rim. And in both instances, he was right—until the last 5:00 of the game. After Cade's comment, Remington doubted himself. The basket looked like it was the size of the drain in his bathroom sink, and everybody who guarded him was on the NBA All-Defensive team.

Chapter 16

Remington couldn't understand what happened. How could one little comment by the most selfish player he had ever known have such a huge effect on him? Why did he let Cade get into his head that way? Remington was the same player for the twenty-seven minutes before the comment, but all he could focus on was that maybe he was someone else—a ball hog who his teammates didn't like. Then he started to doubt if the ball would go in, so he didn't shoot. And of course, he thought about Cade yelling at him again if he shot it, even though Cade had apologized and told him to keep shooting.

Remington hadn't realized it before, but he was starting to see something in a whole new light. The best defender that Remington had ever played against and would ever play against was his own mind, his own conscience. By letting Cade get into his head, he let Cade's words affect him in a negative way. While it could be attributed to Cade, it was Remington who let Cade's words in there and let them affect him. So while it was Cade's fault that Cade behaved the way he did, it was Remington's fault that he let Cade affect him so much.

Ultimately, nobody could ever stop Remington the way Remington could. He needed to see Cade's words affecting his confidence as an opponent that he could beat. He needed to see them the same way he saw players that he could beat off the dribble or shoot over anytime he wanted. But that was a lot easier said than done. Still, now that he could see how Cade's words contributed to his lack of confidence in a tangible way, he might be able to attack it.

Remington said sarcastically, "Thanks, Nick. I can always count on you to build me up and help me feel better about myself."

Nick said, "It's what I do, man," and all three of them laughed as they got to the bus. When Remington stepped onto the bus, the entire bus started cheering. Comments of "Great game, Rem!" filled the air. Embarrassed at the attention, Remington smiled and tried to find the first seat he could dive into, so he wouldn't have to show his embarrassment. As he looked for a seat, he saw Cade looking at him. Cade was not smiling or cheering. He was just staring at Remington. Remington dropped into a seat three rows in front of Cade next to Mike Visteen. Mike fist-bumped him and said, "Awesome job, Rem."

Remington said, "Thanks, Mike." He put his headphones on and stared out the front window of the bus.

Ideas to Consider:

- What is Remington worried about that his teammates might think of him? What is Nick and Tim's response to Remington's concern?

- According to Nick, Remington's unselfishness can sometimes be selfish. How is that possible?

Chapter 17

Remington was glad it was Mike who he was sitting with. They had been friends since 6th grade, but Mike was very quiet, not prone to much conversation. Remington had so many thoughts racing around his head that he didn't want to talk right then. As he sat there staring out the front window listening to hip-hop music in his AirPods, he continued thinking about his confidence issues. As the bus pulled away from the school and turned out onto the highway to head back to Discovery, Remington's thoughts took him back to last year when he was a sophomore playing on the varsity. That was the first time he started struggling with his confidence.

His lack of confidence last year was always brought about in one of two ways—Cade's comments and actions or Coach Brooks' comments. Cade's were obvious. He was upset whenever Remington was getting glory from his teammates, coaches, and fans. He didn't like that the attention was not on him. Just like when Remington had just stepped onto the bus. While it was embarrassing, it felt good to Remington to hear his teammates treat him that way—until he saw Cade's face. Then, all the joy and fun of the moment was sucked right out of him. That was the hold that Cade had on him.

While Cade's largest impact on Remington's confidence started last year, his impact on Remington had actually started in middle school. While he and Cade didn't play on the same team, Cade made sure that Remington knew that Cade was better than everyone else, including Remington. Remington never sought to be better than Cade, or anyone else for that matter.

Growing up, Remington's dad taught him a lot of things about basketball and life. One of those was that you should never try to be better than other people. The only person you should compare yourself to is you. His dad would say, "The only true competition we have that matters is the one with ourselves. If we can compete against our potential best, then we will focus on what truly matters—improving to be the best that we can be, not improving to be better than someone else. We don't have control over others, so it is pointless to try to be better than them. But we do have control over ourselves. If you can work today to be better than the person you were yesterday, that is all you need to do. The rest will take care of itself."

Remington's dad's words instilled in him not to care who was the best, and that all that mattered was if you were your best you. If you were the best you could be, then you had taken control of the things you could control. You weren't concerned with outside, external forces that you had no control over.

Cade, on the other hand, was all about comparisons with others. He constantly was telling people that he was better than that guy or this guy. Most people just blew it off as Cade being Cade. They knew Cade was good, and that, in fact, he was better than a lot of guys. He didn't need to tell anyone that; they could see it for themselves. But the more he talked about it, the more he turned people off.

As the years went on, people started drifting further away from Cade because he was so arrogant. Some of his teammates even secretly hoped he would fail, hoping that might shut him up. But even when he did fail, he kept talking, making excuses, and blaming things out of his control for what happened. He would tell people he was hurt, or that the ref wouldn't call anything, or that the other player got lucky, or how it was a teammate's fault. It was never that the other player was better or that Cade needed to work on a certain aspect of his game.

Also, while basketball is a team game, it never seemed to be for Cade. It was always about the other player, not the other team. Cade saw every game as a one-on-one game between him and whoever guarded him. The only time he focused on the team was on his own team and only when they lost. Whenever they lost, it was everybody else's fault. He would tell his teammates things like: "You need to work harder," or "You need to get me the ball." Each statement started out with, "You need to..." He never took responsibility for the results or for his role in it.

Since Remington didn't care about comparing himself with anyone else and because Cade seemed so consumed by it, Remington didn't fight it. He actually kind of fed into it. He knew it was important to Cade, so when they started playing together in high school, Remington would do what he could to help Cade have success. He knew that if Cade played well, the chances of

Chapter 17

the team winning were much better, and that was all that mattered to Remington. So he fed the ball to Cade a lot.

As Remington grew throughout his sophomore year, both physically and as a player, his skill levels started to increase at a rapid rate. He had always been a good shooter, but he didn't shoot it all that much last season. But as the season went on and Remington was shooting it better and better, he started to shoot more. That was when Cade first started to rip into him for shooting. Whether he made it or missed it, Remington would hear Cade saying, "Come on, Rem. Pass the ball."

Each time Cade would say something like that, Remington couldn't believe it. Nobody passed the ball to open teammates more than Remington, and nobody received more of his passes than Cade. "How can he say that to me?" Remington thought. "I'm always passing the ball and usually to him.

In a game against Centennial late in the season last year, Remington got on a roll. In the last three minutes of the third quarter, he hit two three-pointers in a row, drove the lane and scored and got fouled for an old-fashioned three-point play, and hit a free-throw line pull-up jumper at the buzzer—11 points in just over three minutes! The gym was going crazy, and Remington was sky-high. His play had been improving all season, and this stretch was the best he had played all year.

As he was running back to the bench Cade came up alongside him with the strangest look in his eyes. He leaned in close, kind of cutting Remington off so as to slow him down to a walk and said, "Who do you think you are? Pass the ball, you frickin' ball-hog. I'm wide open out there and you're jackin' up shots left and right. Get me the ball!"

Remington was crushed. Here he was having the moment of his basketball life, and Cade was destroying it. As he sat on the bench and received all kinds of congratulations and high-fives, he awkwardly smiled. He was upset by what Cade said, and he couldn't shake it. He struggled to focus on what Coach Brooks was saying, but one thing he heard was that Remington was hot and that he needed to keep looking for his shot. He was so conflicted. He wanted to be excited about that, but Cade's comments had him reeling.

The first time down the court to start the quarter, his defender slipped, and Remington had another open look at a three. He passed it up. He saw Cade flashing through the lane and passed it to him. Cade forced a tough, guarded turn-around jump shot that clanged off the back of the iron. The next time down Remington had an open drive to the basket. He had a chance to go up and finish and try to draw a foul, but he chose to kick it out to Cade in the corner for a three-pointer. Cade shot an airball.

The rest of the fourth quarter was pretty much that way. Remington only took two shots, both of them open layups. He finished the game with 19 points, which was a great night for anyone, but he stopped being the player he had been in the third quarter. Cade finished with 18 points, but 12 of them had come in the first two-and-a-half quarters of the game. In the fourth quarter he took eight shots and missed all of them. His only points in the quarter came on two free throws. After leading by six going into the fourth quarter, the Wolves ended up losing to Centennial by eight.

In the last few games that season, Remington was a shell of the player he had been in the third quarter. While he still handled the ball and passed it well, he shot only a handful of times in each game. Other than Cade, his teammates kept telling him to shoot it, but he kept passing up open shots. The opponents saw this, too, so they started laying off of him and keying on his passes, which was his greatest skill.

Remington threw passes that didn't seem possible. People wondered how he saw his teammate to whom he threw some of the passes and how he fit it through that space to him. As cliché as it was, people would say, "He has eyes in the back of his head." Some would then add, "and on the side and top and underneath. That kid sees things nobody else can."

Because of his ability to pass the ball unlike others, Remington sometimes pushed the envelope on what would be considered an "acceptable" pass by coaches. Del loved how well Remington got the ball to open players. However, he struggled with some of the passes that he threw that were risky. Remington occasionally threw behind-the-back and drop-through-the-legs passes. Usually, they were on the money. He didn't do them to be fancy. He did them because in that moment, they were the best way to get the ball to his open teammate.

However, there were times when his passes were not successful. At those moments, Del would yell out, "No fancy passes. Make it simple!"

Remington would think, "That wasn't fancy. That was the right pass for that spot. I just didn't put it in the right place." Of course, he would never say that, but it bothered him.

Chapter 17

Later he would think, "I am averaging over three assists and less than two turnovers a game. That's a positive assist-to-turnover ratio. And the assists are the ones that our guys actually score on. How many more do I get to them when they don't actually make the basket? I'm also human. I'm going to have an occasional turnover. But I'm also going to put the ball in our guys' hands in great spots most of the time."

Whenever Coach Brooks would say something about it, Remington would nod his head. From then on, he would play much more conservatively and not push the boundary. Unfortunately, this led him to lose his confidence and not be as aggressive in all phases of his offense. He would get tentative and doubt his dribbling abilities, so he wouldn't attack the basket, another strong suit of his.

Here he was, a key member of a basketball team hesitant to shoot, pass, or dribble. In the final two regular season games last year, he was no longer the player he had been before. He was now just taking up space on the floor. He would catch a pass and either freeze or immediately pass it to a wide-open teammate. He didn't want to shoot because of Cade's comments, he didn't want to pass because of Coach Brooks's comments, and he didn't want to drive because he was so worried about making any kind of mistake that might make either of them upset. He had lost all of his confidence, and he had no clue how to find it again.

Unfortunately, Remington's lack of confidence carried on into the Divisional Tournament. He was nervous playing in his first tournament, and the more he thought about it, the worse it got. He played tentatively and scared. He just couldn't shake Cade's and Coach's comments, and he shrank in the moment. For all the promise he had shown as the season went on, he couldn't get it going in the tournament.

At the same time, Cade continued being Cade. Focused only on himself, he tried way too hard to "be the man." The seniors on last year's team had grown tired of him and his selfishness, and they let him know in no uncertain terms that they were not going to let him hijack the end of their season. But Cade didn't care. He knew that the tournament would have its share of college scouts there watching some of the seniors and juniors from other teams. He needed to get on their radars, so he needed to score. He shot it any time he felt the slightest bit open. He looked off open teammates in order to "get his."

There were a couple of problems with this strategy. One was that the majority of the college scouts Cade was figuring would be there weren't there because the game was between two of the weakest teams in the division, neither of whom had any players that had shown too much potential for college greatness. The second problem with his strategy was that he shot so much and missed so much that there was nothing impressive about his play.

While Cade finished with 12 points in the first game, he shot 4 for 21, a dismal 19% shooting percentage. He also had no assists. In fact, once the ball was in the front-court, and the Wolves were running their offense, he rarely passed the ball at all. They lost 63-51. At the hotel that night, two of the seniors pulled Cade into their room and told him that he better change his ways in the next day's game against Highline or there would be hell to pay. Cade was shaken by that. He didn't know exactly what they meant they would do, but he was worried. While he was a strong kid and could handle himself, he was still worried.

However, you wouldn't have been able to tell anything was different the next day with the way Cade played. Highline was a team in the Wolves' conference, and they were very similar to the Wolves in terms of record and talent. Cade knew in his mind that he was better than anyone on that team, and he was going to prove it. While he started out passing and playing a somewhat team-oriented game in the first half, he went into full-blown "Cade Mode" in the second half. He rarely looked to any of his teammates, no matter what they or Del said to him. By the end of the quarter, Highline was up by 13 points, and nothing the Wolves had tried worked. The fourth quarter saw much of the same kind of action, and the Wolves' season ended in a 58-49 defeat. Cade shot the ball better, finishing with 14 points going 5-for-12.

Ironically, though, it was all for naught again, as scouts don't often go to Loser-Out tournament games if they don't have a specific player or players they are looking at. So, while Cade was being Cade trying to impress college scouts, all he ended up doing was help put an end to his team's season. The other irony, of course, is that by him shooting them out of the tournament, he also shot away his own chances of being seen by scouts because his season was over. He would have to wait until the summer and then his senior year to get any looks from scouts. Time was running out on Cade to get his shot at playing D1 college ball. At this rate, he'd be lucky to get a shot at playing college ball at any level. He just didn't realize it yet.

Chapter 17

Ideas to Consider:

- This chapter focuses on the prior year when Remington was a sophomore. What did Cade do that caused Remington to play tentatively? What did Coach Brooks do that led to the same thing?
- What lessons are here for you as a player like Remington, a player like Cade, or a coach like Coach Brooks? How can understanding their behaviors help you in any similar situations you may encounter?

Chapter 18

As Remington sat there on that bus thinking back to last year and how it all ended, he felt like he was re-living those moments all over again. He didn't like it. He didn't like to think of Cade treating him that way. He didn't like how poorly he played as last season wound down and how poorly he played at the Divisional Tournament. A part of him felt like that was 100 years ago, but another part of him was feeling those same thoughts as if they just happened.

Remington knew this was a different year, and that he was a different player now. But he also knew that he could easily lapse back into that player if he wasn't careful, and that he had done that at times during this season, even in tonight's game. He knew that he needed to shake that kind of mindset and be the player he had become this year—a strong, confident player who could take over games with his ballhandling, passing, shooting, and leadership.

As he sat there staring out the front window of the bus, he knew that his success hinged on flushing his confidence issues from Cade's and Coach's words. When he did that, he was really good. But Remington also knew that when he let the self-doubt creep in and when he let others' words take hold of him, he was just another player, average at best. Remington thought about Nick and Tim's words to him on their way out to the bus. Just like when he was struggling with Cade last year, their words were just what he needed to hear.

But Nick and Tim weren't done yet. All three of their locker room lockers at Sacajawea were in the same area. After the team's practice the following Monday, Nick started in on Remington saying, "Rem, you need to shoot it more in games like you were in practice tonight. Your jumper was wet."

Tim added, "Yeah, you were killing it, man. You couldn't miss. But that also opens up your drives to the hoop. Then when you drive and we spot up in the corner, our defenders leave us to help on you, so we're sitting there wide open for 3s. Keep doing both, dude. Knock down your jumpers, and look for your drives and kicks."

Nick came back with, "Yeah, he's right. I love it when you attack the rim cuz I know I'm gonna' get good looks when you drive and then throw one of those sick passes. That's how so many of us get our chances to score, Rem. Don't worry about what Coach says. He's a coach. He's gotta' say that stuff about fancy passes. But seriously, what's he gonna' do? It's not like he's going to take you out when you're playing so well."

Before and after practice each night was like that. Nick and Tim would tag-team Remington trying to bring back the Remington they had played with for most of the last six years. They started pulling Billy, Brian, and Mike into the mix. Each would offer a comment about how they liked it when he shot, passed, or drove to the hole. They all knew that if he played the way he plays when he's feeling good about things, they would all be better because of it.

Remington started feeling better with each comment he heard. While he would probably continue to worry about what Cade and Coach said, his biggest concern had always been if the rest of his teammates actually felt the same way. He didn't want people to think he was ball hog or a showboat, but if the rest of the guys were cool with him playing the way he did, he felt a lot better.

While eating lunch with Jenny one day that week, Remington told her how he didn't know why he struggled so much with Cade's words. "I shouldn't let it bother me. Cade is just a jerk at times when he's playing, and I need to realize that it's not me, it's him."

Jenny said, "'At times'?! You mean he's always a jerk, don't you?"

"No, I don't," said Remington. "He's actually really nice to me here in school. You've heard him. He likes to joke and laugh when we're here in school."

"Yeah, I know that," she said. "But you said he's a jerk 'at times when he's playing.' I'm just saying that it sure seems like he always is that way when he's playing, not just 'at times.'"

As Remington grabbed a few French fries and dipped them into his ketchup, he said, "Yeah, I guess you're right. It's hard to remember him not being that way. I mean, he's had his moments where he seems to be a great guy out on the court, just like he does in here at lunch or in the halls. But for the most part, he's just so hard to play with." He bit into his fries.

Jenny said, "Rem, I don't know what I can say that will make it better. Cade is who he is. Everyone knows it. You know it. Your teammates know it. Your coaches know it. All of us in the crowd know it. I wonder if his parents even know it."

"I doubt that," said Remington. "I'm sure his dad doesn't know it. He's the reason Cade acts that way. When Cade was little, his dad did everything he could to make Cade be 'the man.' He always told Cade's teammates not to shoot it and to get the ball to Cade for the shot. He once took Bruce Popovich out of a game because he shot an open layup instead of kicking it out to Cade in the corner for a 3!"

"No way," said Jenny. "You're kidding."

"As far as I know, it's true," said Remington. "Bruce said that after he made his layup, he's running down the floor, and he sees Tyler Murphy—you remember, Tyler Murphy? He used to play hoops when we were younger?"

"Yeah, I remember him playing with you guys."

Remington continued, "Cade's dad sends Tyler in for Bruce after Bruce makes his layup. As Tyler goes out on the floor, he tells Bruce, 'Coach is pissed you didn't pass it to Cade.'"

"Seriously?" asked Jenny.

"Yeah," said Remington. "As Bruce walks to the bench, he's thinking, 'I had an open layup, and I made it. How can he be mad at me?' Sure enough, when he gets to the sideline, Cade's dad says, 'I told all of you to find Cade when he's open. He was wide open in the corner.' Bruce says to him, 'But I had a wide-open layup, and I made it.' Cade's dad says to him, 'Yeah, but if you'd have thrown it to Cade, we would have gotten 3 points instead of 2.'"

"Unbelievable," said Jenny.

Remington said, "Yeah, no kidding. That's what Cade has dealt with from his dad his whole life. So, I don't totally blame Cade for being the way he is."

Jenny put her fork down, looked Remington in the eyes and said, "I get it, Rem. Cade has some issues, and they have made him who he is.

But you know what. You have issues, too. Your issues are that you are just too darn nice, and you worry way too much about what everyone else thinks of you. It's a double-edged sword. It's why everyone likes you, why everyone on your team loves playing with you. You're always thinking of them and trying to please them. But while you're worried about pleasing everyone else, you're tearing yourself apart. At some point, you need to get a little more selfish."

"Now you sound like Nick and Tim," said Remington.

"Well then Nick and Tim know what they're talking about," she said. "I don't mean you should be a selfish jerk. I mean think of yourself at times. Make sure that you are doing what you do best and not worry so much about helping everyone else get what they want. I know it's a fine line. Sure, you should be a great teammate, but Rem, every single kid on that team knows you're the best teammate out there. Every. Single. One. They all say it all the time."

Remington nodded his head as Jenny continued. "Think back over the last few years. Have you ever NOT won the "Best Teammate" award on your team?"

Remington quickly scanned his brain, thinking back through his playing days in his sports. "Well, we didn't have awards on some of the teams I played on."

"Fine," she said. "Have you ever NOT won it when your teams have had awards?"

"No," he said.

"Exactly. You need to quit worrying about pleasing everybody else. You please your teammates all the time. But you know what? You're a member of the team, too. You're a teammate as well. You need to start pleasing that teammate, too. The only way you're going to do that is if you quit worrying about Cade and Coach because, let's face it, they're the only ones who ever have a problem with anything you do. Get them out of your head and just go play the way you love to play. Just go do all the great things you do when you play."

Remington looked up at Jenny and said, "You're right." He paused and said, "Thanks, Jenny. I can always count on you to bring me back to where I need to be. I can always count on you to help me through things. You've always been there for me. It's what I love about you."

Remington heard the way that came out, saw the look on Jenny's face, and quickly caught himself and said, "I mean, it's what I love about being friends with you so much. I've always been able to count on you to help me through things. Thanks. You're the best."

Jenny had been startled a bit when Remington said that it was what he loved about her. Was he telling her that he loved her? Oh my. Did he really mean that? But then he quickly changed that to "what he loved about being friends with her."

She thought, "Okay, that's what I figured he meant. Still, maybe he was trying to tell me something." However, all she did was sarcastically say, "Well, somebody has to help you out. Otherwise, you'd be rolled up in the fetal position in the corner of this cafeteria!"

The two of them laughed. Remington was glad she said that. Maybe she hadn't caught his little slip-up where he said it was what he loved about her. He didn't really mean to tell her he loved her. He wasn't sure if that was true or not, at least not in that way. But he did love how much she helped him out and how great a friend she was to him. And he might even love her in the other way, but he wasn't sure. He also knew he didn't have time to think that way now. He had the Divisional tournament to focus on and then, hopefully, the state tournament. He could think about that kind of stuff with Jenny after the season. Right now, his mind was focused on "all-ball, all the time," and he liked it that way.

Ideas to Consider:

- **What did Nick, Tim, and Jenny all do to try to help Remington in this chapter? What can you do like that for one or more of your teammates?**

- **What is Remington's "double-edged sword" that Jenny talks about?**

- **Does your team give out a "Best Teammate" award? Why are awards like "Best Teammate," "Hardest Worker," and "Most Improved" better awards to give to team members than awards like "Best Offense" and "Most Valuable Player"? Think of multiple reasons.**

Chapter 19

The Divisional Tournament started on Wednesday. Because they finished in second place in the west side of the division, the Wolves had a first-round bye, so they didn't play until Thursday. They were scheduled to play against the winner of a Wednesday night game between a couple of lower seeded teams from the east. Those two teams were Buckley and Badlands, two teams from over near the Montana/North Dakota border. Badlands was the team the Wolves lost to in their final Divisional game the previous year. Many of the players back from last season hoped they would get Badlands again, because they wanted to avenge that loss.

They got their wish as Badlands beat Buckley in the Wednesday game. The Wolves were scheduled to play on Thursday afternoon. This was one of the tricky parts of tournament play. Badlands already had a game under their belt at the tournament. They had gotten those first-game jitters out and were used to the floor, the arena, and the atmosphere. For kids playing their first game in this environment, it can be a bit overwhelming until they settle in.

All of this conspired to affect the Wolves in the first quarter of their game against Badlands. Badlands was clicking, and the Wolves were not. Everyone seemed to be just a bit off, a step slow. Nobody could find any rhythm, and when they came to the bench at the end of the first quarter, Badlands was ahead 17–9. The Wolves played tight, and they looked tight on the bench. Del tried to be calm and to make sure that he exuded that.

"Welcome to Divisional Tournament basketball, boys! That was a stinker of a quarter, huh?" he asked sarcastically trying to lighten them up a bit. "Okay, the good news is you got your bad quarter at Divisionals out of the way right away. It happens all the time to good teams, especially when they have to play a team that already played a game. Now we can settle down and start playing our game, the way we know how."

In the second quarter, the Wolves started to look like themselves again. With their press forcing turnovers and Remington leading the way by finding teammates on fast breaks and in the half-court offense, they cut into the lead in the first couple of minutes, tied the game with 2:00 left in the half, and went into the locker room for halftime up 32–27. Cade had 10 points in the first half, 8 of them coming off of assists by Remington. It was a whole different feel than the first quarter.

At halftime, Del stressed the importance of maintaining their discipline, while at the same time putting the pedal to the metal. Now, the tables would be turned a bit. In the second half, Badlands would have been playing their fourth half of basketball in two days, whereas the Wolves were fresher. Badlands and Buckley had gone down to the wire the night before, so all of their key players played a lot of minutes. If the Wolves would keep pushing and pressing, they could wear Badlands down.

That's exactly what happened. While Badlands gave great effort to push themselves, their legs just couldn't sustain what their hearts and minds asked of them. The Wolves' press caused numerous turnovers, leading to many fast break points. With 4:00 left in the game and the Wolves up by 29 points, both teams had all second and third string players on the floor. The next day would be pivotal for the Wolves, as they would be playing to go to Saturday night's championship game, as well as a trip to the state tournament.

Cade ended the game with 18 points and 5 rebounds. However, he only had one assist. As often as he had the ball in his hands, and as much scoring as there was for the Wolves, he should have had more assists. However, he started to revert back to his selfish ways even more in this game. While he could get away with that against a weaker opponent like Badlands, the Wolves would struggle to win if he played that way in their semi-final game against Burlington the next night. Burlington had beaten Bighorn in the game right after the Wolves beat Badlands, so that set up a match between Burlington and Sacajawea in a battle to get into the Divisional Championship game.

While every game is important at the Divisional Tournament, Friday night just has a different feel to it. It is semi-final night. The four teams playing on Friday night know that if they win, they are playing for a chance to win a Divisional Championship, and they are also guaranteed a spot at the state tournament. However, they also know that if they lose on Friday night,

Chapter 19

they have to turn around and play again on Saturday morning in the 3rd/4th place game. The winner of that game would go on to the state tournament, while the loser would have to play again in the early evening to try to win a trip to state. These circumstances made the Friday night games some of the most exciting, pressure-packed games at the tournament.

The Burlington Cougars were a few hours east of Discovery. In the early part of the state's history, Burlington had been established as a railroad town. They were tough, hard-nosed kids descended from tough, hard-nosed railroad people. Ironically, in the even earlier days of Montana, Discovery had also been a railroad town, and it stayed that way up until the 1980s. It, too, had its share of toughness about it, and the number of state championships and runner-up finishes that Sacajawea High had in basketball was a result of some of that toughness. But when the railroad pulled out in the 80s, so did the championships. Oh, there were some good runs that some teams had, a few under Del's dad and under Jim Turner. But the "glory years" of Discovery basketball had been gone for some time.

Del was trying to resurrect them. He was trying to bring back a level of success that Sacajawea High and the Discovery community had not seen in a long time. And so as he prepared to face the "other" railroad town school a few hours away down the same tracks that ran through Discovery, he felt a tingle of excitement, and a whole lot of pressure. He wanted so badly for these kids and this community to have a successful team again. If they could win tonight's game, it would be a huge step towards that.

Burlington proved to be everything Del and the coaching staff thought they would be. Tough, gritty kids who were relentless with their man-to-man pressure, nothing came easily to the Wolves. Right from the opening tip, it was obvious that part of Burlington's game plan was to get into Cade's head. They put their peskiest, most annoying defender, Jimmy Schuster, on Cade. It was as if they were playing a Box-and-1 on Cade, even though the rest of the team was playing man-to-man, too. Schuster just had no responsibility to help off of Cade. He was stuck to Cade like glue. Wherever Cade tried to go, Schuster was in his chest.

Normally, this type of defense will open up the rest of the team. However, Burlington was not normal when it came to their defense. Year in and year out, their coach, Paul Harris, had his kids playing some of the toughest defense in the state. His theory was that you didn't have to have any special talent to play great defense. You just had to have determination, grit, and heart. While he worked on offensive skills with his kids, Coach Harris knew that talented, skilled, offensive players come and go. But if he could get his players to buy into the value of being the best defensive team in the state, then every year they would have a shot at a state championship. So that was the mantra he preached throughout his program, long before players came to the high school as freshmen. It had proven to be a very successful concept.

As the game went on, the more Schuster stuck with Cade, the more frustrated Cade got not touching the ball or only touching it in places where he could do nothing with it. The more frustrated Cade got, the more upset he became at his teammates. Late in the first quarter after the third time down the court without Cade getting the ball, Nick dribbled it off of his foot out of bounds. As the team set up in their press, Cade screamed, "Get me the ball!" at all of them.

Jimmy Schuster smiled. Their plan was working. Cade's frustration fueled Schuster's desire and effort to continue to get under Cade's skin. The more Cade didn't touch the ball the more frustrated he got. He picked up an offensive foul for pushing Schuster off of him. As the referee was reporting the foul to the scorer's table, once again Cade lashed out at his teammates. "Set screens for me! I need the ball, so get me open." Schuster had been assigned to guard selfish, arrogant players before, but this Cade kid was at the top of the list for those traits. He also was the easiest to get frustrated and off of his game.

Still, even with Cade struggling to touch the ball, the rest of the Wolves were handling things well. As a counter to tough hard-nosed man defense, Kevin suggested to Del that the Wolves spread the floor out just a bit more than usual to open up the passing lanes more. Burlington did a nice job of sagging off their men when they didn't have the ball to be able to help each other with dribble drives. But as soon as the ball swung back, those defenders were immediately flying out hard to their men to make the passes difficult.

The Wolves countered by quickly faking a pass to the man out wide. As the defender came flying out to stop that pass, the Sacajawea player would cut to the basket right behind the defender running out to guard him. If the cutter received the pass, he had an open layup or another defender was leaving his man to help on him, which left a teammate open for the shot.

Chapter 19

This strategy worked well for the Wolves. The score was tied 16–16 at the end of the quarter.

The second quarter saw much of the same type of action. Everything was a struggle for Cade. He continued to unravel and yell at his teammates for not getting him the ball. Schuster added to Cade's frustration by saying to him, "I can't believe they won't throw you the ball. It's almost like they don't want you to score. You're too good for them to do that, dude."

Cade said, "No kidding. Happens all the time. They're so selfish. They hate that I'm the best player on the team, so they freeze me out like this."

Schuster looked away so Cade wouldn't see him smile. He thought, "Oh my God, I can't believe how arrogant this guy is. He has no clue. He thinks they're the selfish ones."

The few times that Cade did get his hands on the ball, Schuster was right there with him, and Cade struggled to get around him. He forced up two pull-up jumpers with Schuster on him tight. He hit one of them, and missed badly on the other one. But again, the rest of the Wolves were holding their own, and much like the first quarter, the second quarter was a see-saw affair. Burlington had a four-point lead with :20 left in the half.

With the half winding down, Del had Remington hold the ball for one shot. They set up a play that they had worked on at the beginning of the week, specifically for end of quarter situations. The first read was for Cade to shoot a 3-pointer if he was open. If he was covered, he would hit Nick on a cut or Remington coming off of a screen by Brian. As the play developed Cade caught the ball at the three-point line, but immediately Schuster was up on him. The other two reads were both open, but Cade never even thought about passing. He elevated for the three-pointer with Schuster right there with a hand up to challenge the shot. It was an airball.

More importantly, there was still way too much time left on the clock when he shot it, so Burlington had another chance to score. Because of their positions on the floor when Cade shot it, none of the Wolves were back so as to stop a Burlington player sprinting up the floor. A Burlington player rebounded Cade's airball, turned and immediately heaved a long pass up the court to his teammate streaking toward the basket. That player caught the ball and laid it in the basket just before the buzzer. Burlington was up by six at the end of the first half.

In the locker room, Del immediately tried to accentuate the positives from the first half. "Boys, we're actually playing quite well. That is the toughest defensive team we have faced all season, and yet we're getting good looks against them."

Cade looked up at Del when he heard that and thought, "Are you kidding?! I haven't gotten a good look yet!"

Del continued. "Cade, they are keying on you so much that it's opening up lanes for the other guys. We need you to keep your composure and understand what they are doing to you, but also what you can be doing for them. If you don't force the action, it will help us continue to get good looks. Eventually, they will leave you a bit to help as we keep chipping away at them. Then you will get better looks. However, don't force things once you do get the ball. Get it?"

Cade nodded his head, but all he could think about was how he had only scored two points. He needed to get going. His scoring average was taking a huge hit. If he was going to finish the year up high in the state scoring race, he needed to start doing something about it.

Del continued with defensive adjustments and specific matchups to try to take advantage of. He then asked the team, "Okay, what do you see out there?"

Nick said, "We're getting open on those back-door cuts. If they start laying off a bit because of our open cuts, that should open up some three-pointers. Be ready."

Remington said, "Keep moving, and I'll find you. If they keep overplaying you and you back-door cut, get your hands ready cuz I'm throwing it to you right behind the guy's back."

Del said, "Good points. Anyone else?

Cade couldn't handle it anymore. "Yeah, I got something. Get me the ball! You guys never look for me! How can I score without the ball? If we have any shot at winning this game, you need me to score, too. You're not the only ones out there, you know?"

The team sat in somewhat stunned silence, looking at Cade. Del couldn't believe what he just heard, yet at the same time he could. He could see Nick about to explode on Cade, but he put his hand up and cut him off.

Chapter 19

Del said, "Seriously, Cade? First of all, you're wrong. Your teammates look for you all the time. Secondly, you obviously haven't heard anything I've said because I explained why we can't get you the ball. Schuster is on you like a glove. He is on you like they are running a Box-and-1, but they're playing straight man. He is just not helping off of you at all. That means you're going to get far less touches. It also means your teammates are going to have a lot more looks. Of course, you can't stand that because it means you can't 'be the man.' But it actually is helping us get good looks and helping us compete against their defense."

Cade was looking at the floor, but Del just kept talking. "This half be ready for more of the same. It will be up to you to make a decision. Care more about us winning this game and keep doing what you and we are doing, or care more about you scoring points and start forcing things. I know which choice I want you to make. I know which choice your teammates want you to make. However, you'll be the one who makes the choice. I hope it's the right one."

Del looked at all of them again and said, "All right, everybody up. Hands in." They all put their hands in with Cade in his customary place on the outside of the circle, barely putting his hand near the rest of them. Nick yelled out, "Wolves on three... 1, 2, 3—Wolves!"

Ideas to Consider:

- **Why does Jimmy Schuster say to Cade what he says to him?**
- **What is working for Sacajawea against the Burlington team's defense? Why is that bothering Cade? What is Cade most interested in doing in the second half?**
- **Think ahead as if you were one of the coaches. What do the coaches need to be prepared for in the second half? What are some responses they may need to have ready?**

Chapter 20

To start the second half, Paul Harris did something subtle, yet masterful. He told Jimmy Schuster to start letting Cade catch the ball. Then, once Cade had it, Schuster would get up into his body and make things tough on him. Because Cade was a selfish player and only had three shot attempts in the first half, Paul knew that upon catching it, Cade would start forcing shots.

That's exactly what happened. On the Wolves' first possession, Cade caught the first pass to him out on the wing three feet behind the three-point line. Jimmy had forced him out farther than Cade wanted to be, then laid off him an extra foot, so as to allow him to catch the pass. As Cade caught it and turned, he saw that Jimmy was off of him more than he had been the whole first half. Cade launched a three-pointer, but because he was farther away than usual, the shot fell way short. The next time down, Jimmy allowed Cade to catch the ball at the free throw line but then got right up on him. Cade turned and started to drive around Jimmy, but another Burlington defender stepped over to help on Cade. They knew he wasn't going to pass it, and Cade forced an off-balance running jump shot with a hand in his face that grazed the side of the rim.

Kevin Nixon had been watching the scene play out. A little over a minute into the half, he had figured out what Paul Harris was doing. He told Del, "They're letting Cade catch it now, daring him to shoot. They know he'll force things up since he has had so few shots. We need to tell Cade to swing it on his first and maybe even second catches. Otherwise, their whole defense will be ready to attack him on drives. But if we can catch them after a swing or two of the ball, they won't be in the same position."

Del wondered how Kevin was able to figure that out in such a short amount of time. Sure enough, that's exactly what was playing out. On a dead ball, Del yelled, "Cade! Swing the ball when you catch it. Don't force the action. Let it come to you after things open up a bit." Cade nodded his head, but he had no intention of swinging the ball. He was finally open, and he was going to take advantage of that and put his team on his back and carry them.

As Cade continued to force bad shots, Burlington started to extend their lead. Halfway through the quarter, the Wolves were down by thirteen. Cade had taken all but three of their shots in that span. Del called timeout. As the team came to the bench, Nick yelled at Cade, "Now who's not getting the ball to his teammates?! Pass the frickin' ball, Cade!"

Cade got chest-to-chest with Nick and yelled, "Shut up, Nick! You can't win without me scoring!"

Nick yelled back at him, "Don't you mean *WE* can't win without you scoring, Cade? Or are we the opponent to you, too? And if you call what you're doing scoring, you've got far bigger problems, Cade!"

Del and Kevin separated the two of them and told them to sit down. Paul Harris looked over from in front of his bench and smiled. His plan was working to perfection. Not only was Cade forcing up bad shots, but his teammates were frustrated with him, too.

Del kneeled in front of the bench. "Cade, you're getting open more, aren't you?" Cade nodded. "Do you know why?" Cade looked a little confused. "It's not because you're doing anything different or because we're doing anything different. It's because Schuster is letting you catch it. They want you to catch it, Cade? Do you know why?"

Cade was dumbfounded. "No."

"Because they know you'll do exactly what you've done for the last four minutes—force up every shot you can. You played right into their hands, Cade. They want you to force shots cuz their coach has figured you out. They know you won't pass the ball. Swing the ball when you get it. Their whole defense will have to shift when that happens. When you get it back, there may be a seam to exploit, but if not, swing it again. Either your teammates will be open, or it will create opportunities for you to be open."

Del turned to the rest of the team. "That goes for all of you. The more we swing the ball from one side of the floor to the other, the more we make them work on defense, and the more we open up driving lanes and open shots. Don't take the first shot that presents itself. That's exactly what they want."

For the next four minutes, the Wolves, including Cade, did as Del said, and it worked beautifully. Lanes opened up on the reversal of the ball, and they got open cuts, drives, and jump shots. Cade had six points, all on open drives to the basket after a swing of the ball. By the end of the third quarter, the Wolves had cut the lead to two. Paul Harris looked frustrated as his team came to the bench. The Wolves looked energized. As they were coming to the bench, Kevin told Del, "Be ready for them to go back to playing Cade tight again. Their second half plan just backfired."

Del told the team, "All right, great job! Swinging the ball was the key. Do you see what I mean, Cade? That really disrupted their defense. Now here's the deal. We need to be ready for them to go back to playing Cade tight like in the first half. Cade, get ready for Schuster to be all over you again. They rested him the last three minutes, so he will be fresh. Don't force the action. The rest of you understand that your lanes will be opened up again, especially when you are near Cade. Schuster will not be helping off of Cade, so drive to the side of your man that Schuster is on." Cade couldn't believe it. He finally got a little rhythm going, was finally scoring, and coach was telling him not to force it. He knew better. He knew his team needed him to attack.

As the two teams broke their huddles and headed out to the floor, Schuster waited at the free throw line. As Cade headed to a wing, Schuster did not go stand very close to him. Cade thought, "Coach doesn't know what he's talking about. This guy isn't on me tight. I'm going to still have good looks." Cade was excited to get the ball and do his thing.

As Remington received the inbounds pass and started to set up the offense, he saw Schuster laying off of Cade. He thought, "Wow! I guess they're not going to stick him so tight. Remington fired the initial entry pass to Cade, and he made his cut to the opposite wing. As he did this, Remington's man followed the pass to Cade. He and Schuster immediately double-teamed Cade. Cade was already putting the ball on the floor when the trap occurred, and Remington's man stole the ball. He had an open lane down the court for an easy lay-up.

On the ensuing possession, Remington entered the ball to Nick. Nick found that Schuster was laying off Cade again, this time at the point. Nick passed to Cade and cut to the basket. Nick's man followed his pass to Cade to apply the trap. Nick was open on his cut. Cade had other plans, though.

Chapter 20

He knew that the trap was coming quickly and that Schuster was closing out on him. Instead of passing to the open Nick, he immediately launched a long three-pointer. It missed badly. Cade dropped his head in disappointment. With Cade not running back, Schuster had sprinted downcourt and received a long pass for another easy layup.

Del yelled, "Cade, don't force it!" He might as well have been talking to a deaf person.

Cade didn't want to hear it. He knew better. "How does Coach not see it? They're letting me catch it. I'm open."

Each possession saw more of the same. Cade was open on the catch. Schuster laid off of him until a teammate came to trap him. Cade forced something either before the trap occurred or after they were both on him. It didn't matter. Both choices spelled disaster for the Wolves.

Halfway through the quarter, Burlington was up by fourteen. Del subbed Mike Visteen for Cade after Cade forced up another bad shot. Cade couldn't believe Del was taking him out at this key moment in the game. He said, "Coach, what are you doing? We're still in this!"

Del said, "Yeah, I know, Cade. We are still in this. But you're not. You haven't done one thing this quarter that we talked about in the huddle. You have forced up bad shot after bad shot. You're killing us out there."

Cade dropped his head, mumbled something under his breath, and walked to the end of the bench. Del sat down, turned to Kevin, and said, "Did you hear what he said?"

"No, I didn't hear it clearly," said Kevin.

Del was boiling inside. He struggled to put his thoughts together. He knew he needed to focus on the floor and on his team out there, but he couldn't shake Cade out of his head. Fortunately, Remington was in front of him asking what defense he wanted them in. Del snapped out of it to tell him "straight man-to-man."

Unfortunately for the Wolves, although they cut into the lead momentarily after Cade went out, Burlington finally pulled away at the end of the game, beating the Wolves 59–47. It was the Wolves' lowest point total all season. Burlington had worked their defensive game plan on Cade almost to perfection.

The locker room was quiet when Del walked in. He struggled to find the right words. He knew he shouldn't say too much that was negative. His team was hurting, and they were one win away from going to the state tournament, and one loss away from their season being over. Waiting for them in the 3rd/4th place game was their archrival Gallatin, who they lost to a couple weeks before, and who lost their semifinal game earlier. Gallatin—the team that was in their heads more than any other, and the team who they should have beaten both times they played them but didn't due to Cade's selfishness. Del had to find a way to help the boys get past tonight's game and move to believing they could beat Gallatin and get to the state tournament.

"Boys, we need to learn from this, flush it, and move on." Del looked around. "Burlington had a great game plan. Gallatin was watching, and they will probably do the same thing." Del looked at Cade. "Cade, get ready for more of the same treatment tomorrow. If you react the way you did tonight, though, we will have a similar result, and our season will be over."

Cade had a glassy-eyed look on his face. Del wondered if Cade was hearing what he was saying. He continued. "The difference will be that if I see you forcing the action again like you did tonight, instead of playing with your teammates, I won't keep you on the floor." Some of the players were already questioning if that would happen when Del turned back to them.

"I let you all down tonight. I made poor decisions tonight." He did not want to call Cade out in front of the team again. The time for that was over. He had tried to communicate with Cade individually, and that didn't work. He had tried to call him out in front of his team, and that hadn't worked either. The only thing left to do was to sit Cade if he wouldn't be a team player. Del needed to reward the right behaviors and punish the wrong ones. He knew he should have been doing that all year long. But he had felt they needed Cade on the floor to win. He wanted to see if Cade would come around. Truth be told, he also didn't want to have to deal with Cade's attitude or potential outbursts.

It had worked at times during the season, but as the season went on, Cade drifted back to being the Cade of old. Del addressed it a bit, but not enough. The greatest motivator of all, especially for players like Cade, was the bench. But Del had not used the bench enough this year. As good as the Wolves were, they had beaten so many teams by convincing margins, he didn't have to sit Cade out all that much, other than when they were blowing teams out, and he was playing the second and third string players.

But when they were in tight games and Cade played his old, selfish way, Del had not pulled him out enough. Now the team was suffering because of it. Del knew the divisional tournament was not the time that he should start sending messages to players by sitting them out for bad behavior. That should have happened long ago. But he had put himself and the team into this position, and tomorrow he might just have to do that. Besides, it wasn't necessarily sending Cade a message as much as it was doing the smart thing. If Cade couldn't play the way he needed to in order for the team to be successful, he needed to sit. Del would do that with anyone else, so why not do that with Cade?

Ideas to Consider:

- **What did Paul Harris, the coach from Burlington, do in the third quarter and fourth quarter that caused Cade to force shots he shouldn't have? What made Harris think strategies like that would work?**
- **Some people might say that Paul Harris outcoached Del in this game. Is that what happened, or is there a deeper situation happening here that explains the outcome of the game better?**

Chapter 21

The next day, as they all sat in the locker room before the Gallatin game, Del was going over the plan. On defense, they would full-court press, trying to put great pressure on Gallatin's guards. He was hoping to force a lot of up-tempo action, with Remington and Nick bringing the ball up the floor, looking ahead to Cade, Billy, and Brian for transition buckets. In the half court, they needed to be patient against what he assumed would be Gallatin's defensive game plan that would mimic what Burlington did the night before. He drew a few plays and sets that he figured Gallatin would employ that hurt them the first two times they played Gallatin.

Del was finished with the strategy talk. He turned away from the white board, still holding onto the marker. "Boys, it's tough to beat a team that is similar to you in talent and ability three times in a season. And, quite honestly, we're more talented than Gallatin. But both times we played them, we didn't play all that well, and we certainly didn't play well together." Del looked right at Cade. He knew he was doing it again, saying that they had played selfishly, instead of saying Cade had played selfishly, but he didn't need to go there right now. He figured by staring right at Cade as he said it, they would all understand what he meant. He just wanted everyone focused on one thing—playing together.

Del continued. "That can't happen tonight. If we play OUR game and we play it," he turned to the board and wrote while he spoke, "'TOGETHER,' they cannot beat us a third time."

He paused to let that sink in. He then said, "If you remember the first night of the year, I wrote that word on the board for us. I said that word would be the key to our season this year. I said that we MUST be a together team if we are going to-" and just like the first night he turned to the white board and wrote as he said it, "GET TO STATE."

He let the words hang in the air, let them think of getting to the state tournament. "That became our goal, our focus, our guiding light this year."

Chapter 21

He pointed at the board as he said, "GET TO STATE—TOGETHER!"

He paused for a moment and then continued. "Well boys, this is it. This is what we've been aiming for all year long. This has been our goal from that very first night in the locker room. It's up to all of us to go out there and make it happen." He again pointed to the word *TOGETHER* on the board. "If we do that, we will be playing in the state tournament in Great Falls next weekend."

"What happens next week is gravy, though. It's icing on the cake. Our #1 goal has always been getting there. Once we're there, we'll worry about how to deal with it. Right now, there is one focus and one focus only." Del turned toward the board again, pointed, and said, "Get to State." Turning back to the boys he said, "And how are we going to get there?"

"Together," they responded.

Del raised his voice, "How?"

"TOGETHER!"

"HOW?"

"TOGETHER!!!" The boys all jumped to their feet, clapping their hands.

Del yelled, "Let's go! Let's do this! Let's get out there and give it all we've got. Hands in."

The team put their hands up above Del's head, and Del yelled, "Together on three... 1, 2, 3," and they all yelled, "TOGETHER!" They ran out of the locker room door to warm up.

When the game started, Gallatin did not employ the same tactic that Burlington had. Del and Kevin were shocked. Instead, Gallatin employed the same strategies that had been successful for them the first two times they played, alternating between a straight man-to-man defense and a trapping half-court zone defense. Neither was working all that well.

The Wolves jumped out to a six-point lead five minutes into the game. Remington was finding open teammates on the break and in the half-court, and they were all getting good looks off of his drives and kick-out passes. By the end of the quarter, he already had four assists, three of them to Cade, who had seven points. Though Remington hadn't scored a point, he was ecstatic as they came to the bench. "Let's go! Let's keep this up! Keep stepping to those open spots, and I'll keep finding you. Be ready to go back door on them now, cuz as well as you guys are shooting, I bet they'll start closing out on you quick."

Del echoed Remington's words about back door cuts, and then said, "Be ready for them to switch things up a bit. As well as we're handling their man and their trap, I wouldn't be surprised if they do something different this quarter. Whatever they throw at you, relax. Don't panic, just adjust to it. Don't force anything that's not there." While Del was talking to everyone, he was thinking specifically of Cade.

Sure enough, Gallatin came out with the same defensive strategy on Cade that Burlington had used the day before. They stuck Aaron Trout on Cade. Trout was another one of those hard-nosed kids that loved the challenge of stopping a team's best scorer. Remington immediately recognized what was happening and at the next dead ball stepped over to Cade. "Cade, Trout is on you. He is going to be in your grill everywhere you go. Don't force the action. We will all be open for you to find us."

Cade nodded his head and said "Got it," but inside he was thinking, "Screw you. I am not looking for you, dude. That kid can't stop me. I'm already tearing it up. I am not going to stop attacking now, not when I've got it going like this."

Unfortunately, Cade's actions followed his thoughts. While the lanes were opened up even more for his teammates, Cade was covered tightly by Trout. Just like in the Burlington game, he was struggling to get open. The few times that he did receive a pass, he refused to look for his open teammates. He either drove into double-teams and forced a contested shot, or he shot a contested deep three-pointer before Trout could get up on him closely. He missed each time, and Gallatin capitalized with fast-break points of their own.

Fortunately, Remington recognized what was happening. Instead of forcing action to Cade, Remington found the rest of his teammates. He had told his teammates to look for the backdoor cuts. However, because Gallatin had switched their defense, all of the defenders other than Trout were sagging back in the lane to be ready to help on Cade's drives. This left the rest of the team open behind the three-point line. Remington found them on swing passes and drives, and he continued to rack up the assists. The game was tied at 32 at the half.

Chapter 21

The feeling in the locker room was positive for the most part. While they had lost the lead during the second quarter, they felt good that they had battled back to tie it. Their shots were falling, they were playing good defense, and they were handling the way Gallatin was playing them. Cade had stopped forcing bad shots, and Del was pleased overall.

"All right, that's a decent half. They switched things up on us there, and I think, for the most part, we adjusted well. Cade, Trout is playing you like Schuster did last night. Remember the problems you had last night forcing the action. That's not gonna' cut it tonight.

"If you want to get open more, go screen for your teammates. I know that sounds backwards, that they should be screening for you, and of course, they should be. But as we all know, more often than not, the guy who gets open on a screen is the screener because the defense focuses on the guy receiving the screen. See if screening for someone frees you up. If Trout stays tight on you, though, that should free up your teammate. If you do get a pass but he's up on you tight, swing the ball. Don't force the action!"

The team all heard Del, but they all wondered if Cade had heard him. They liked the plan, and they had seen it work throughout the year. Remington had hit the screener with a pass so many times, he started looking for him first and the man coming off the screen second. He just hoped Cade would actually try it.

The third quarter started and to his credit, Cade set two great screens on the first two possessions. Both of them created wide open looks for teammates, one for Nick and one for Brian. Each of them knocked down a jump shot, and the Wolves went up by four points. The next time down, though, Cade stood on the wing and called Nick to screen for him. Nick set a great screen on Trout. Nick's man switched to help on Cade cutting to the basket, but Trout knew his job was to stop Cade, so he stayed with Cade, too. Nick was wide open. Remington looked at Cade and saw both men on him. While looking at Cade, Remington hit Nick for a wide-open three-pointer. The Wolves were now up seven. Gallatin called a quick timeout.

They were pumped as they jogged to the bench. Nick high-fived Remington and said, "Nice pass!"

Remington responded, "Keep shooting, man. You're hot!"

Cade stepped up to both of them before they got to the huddle and said,

"Get me the ball. I thought I'm supposed to be the one you look for when I screen. I did that twice, and you didn't throw it to me. Then he screens for me, and you throw it to him. Get ME the ball!"

At this point they were to the team's huddle, so neither of them responded. But Nick and Remington both just looked at each other and rolled their eyes. While they knew how selfish Cade was, they still couldn't believe it sometimes. Here they had just run the offense exactly how Coach had said they should and hit their first three shots while holding Gallatin scoreless, and all Cade could think of was that he didn't get the ball. Unbelievable!

In the huddle, Del said, "Nice job. That's the way to run that screen action, Cade. That got us three wide open looks." The look on Cade's face was not one of happiness for what he had just done, and Del made a mental note of it. Del continued, "Keep looking for that. Cade keep setting screens for your teammates. Rem, keep reading which guy is open off that screen."

Kevin Nixon stepped to Del after the huddle broke. "I don't think Cade is all too thrilled with the strategy. We better keep an eye on him. As well as that first minute went, this could go south in a hurry if he doesn't buy in."

"Yeah, I know. How does he not get it?"

Gallatin employed a different tactic after the timeout. Much like Burlington had Schuster do in the second half, Trout was now laying off Cade, enticing the Wolves to throw him the pass. The moment he received it, Trout was up on him, and the rest of the team got into the driving lanes. Just like the night before, all Cade saw was that he was open. He didn't see how quickly they were closing him down. For the next three possessions, each time he caught it, he tried to drive, only to be met by another Gallatin defender. He forced a shot the first time, turned it over the second time, and forced a shot the third time. Just like that, Gallatin had tied the game back up.

Del yelled, "Cade, quit forcing it! Swing the ball. You'll get it back in a better position."

Cade just looked at Del and turned back to the action on the court. The next few possessions saw each team trade baskets and stops. When Cade got it, he swung it to open teammates and then made his cuts. He created space for open shots for teammates. However, that's not what he wanted. He

Chapter 21

needed to score. This might be his final high school game, and there might be scouts in the stands. He needed to show them what he could do.

The next three possessions saw Cade forcing the action instead of including his teammates. He managed to score a tough, contested layup, making a shot that he should have never taken. He missed badly and turned it over on the other two possessions. Gallatin was now up by four. Del looked at Kevin. "What do you think?"

"I'd say get him out of there. He's not doing what you said, and he's killing our flow."

Del was thinking hard about his options. He had said yesterday that he would pull Cade if he played this way. However, he struggled taking Cade off the floor in key moments. He knew Cade was prepared to play in big moments, but he wasn't sure if the rest of his guys were. As Del was thinking about what to do, Brian Johnson got a defensive rebound and kicked it out to Remington. Remington started the break, and saw Cade streaking up the floor. However, Remington recognized that Gallatin had two defenders back, one of whom was running right alongside Cade. Remington couldn't get him the ball. He looked ahead and hit Tim on the other side of the court. Cade threw his hands up in the air in disgust and yelled, "Get me the ball!"

Tim caught it, held it as he looked for an open teammate, and then swung it back out to Remington. As Remington caught the ball, he put two fingers in the air and yelled out, "2!"

The players moved to their spots to run the play. It was designed to get Brian either a layup or jump shot. The first pass would go to Cade. Brian would back screen for Remington and then either roll to the basket or pop to the three-point line depending on what his defender did. Remington threw it to Cade, who was open on the wing. Brian set the screen for Remington. Both men went with Remington on his cut to the basket, and Brian popped to the three-point line wide open.

Cade never even looked Brian's way. The moment he caught the ball, he swept it low across his body and took off on a dribble drive. He had just gotten around Trout, when Remington's man recognized what was happening and stepped over into Cade's path. He positioned himself perfectly in front of Cade, and Cade plowed into him. The referee blew his whistle and signaled a charge on Cade. Cade jumped up and yelled, "Oh NO! He wasn't set!"

As the referee started towards the scorer's table to report the foul, Cade yelled, "That's terrible," and he threw the ball to the floor hard. It bounced up well over his head. The referee turned towards Cade, blew his whistle, and put his hands together in the shape of a T. Cade had just received a technical foul for his outburst. He started towards the official, but Remington stepped in front of him. "Calm down, Cade," said Remington.

Cade kind of shoved Remington aside and said, "Shut up, Rem. Get out of my way."

Remington stood his ground, staying between Cade and the official, sort of guiding Cade towards the bench. "Not gonna' do that, Cade. We can't afford to have you do any more stupid crap. This game is too close to let you get another technical."

Cade didn't push it anymore, and he headed down the floor. However, by now, Del had sent Mike Visteen to the scorer's table to report for Cade. Cade saw that and said, "Coach, I'm okay. I'm fine. Leave me in. I won't do that anymore."

As Mike was buzzed into the game and Cade started walking to the bench, Del said, "You're right, Cade. You won't do that anymore. Sit down."

Gallatin hit the two technical foul free throws and scored on the subsequent possession to take an eight-point lead with 2:30 left in the quarter. Over the next two-and-a-half minutes, though, the Wolves started playing like a team again. Mike Visteen gave them a nice little boost on offense, and the press caused a couple of turnovers that led to layups. The Wolves cut the lead to two by the end of the quarter. The fourth quarter was set up to be a real barn-burner.

Ideas to Consider:

- Coach Brooks says it's hard for a team to beat another team of similar talent three times in a season. Do you think that is true? If so, why would it be that way? If not, why would he say that?
- What makes a player like Cade so frustrating to coach or to play with? Is there anything coaches or teammates can do to help that player change?

Chapter 22

As the teams headed to the bench at the end of the third quarter, Cade stepped over to Del and said, "Coach, I'm ready to go," and he started walking to the scorer's table to report in.

Del looked at him and said, "No you're not, Cade. Stand in the huddle with your teammates."

The five players who were playing at the end of the quarter took their seats on the bench, and Del kneeled in front of them. "All right. Nice job of fighting back. Mike, great job of finding your spots out there. They're going to start keying on your jump shots, so be ready to shot fake and drive. If you can get to the hole, great. But if not, be ready to kick it to an open teammate. Get it?"

Mike nodded his understanding and said, "Okay."

Del continued, "Rem, keep finding guys, but make sure you look for your shot, too. You passed up some good, open looks out there to get it to teammates. I love your unselfishness, but you need to be selfish at times. We need you to score, too." Nick, sitting next to Remington, smiled, leaned over, and said, "Sound familiar?"

Cade, barely listening to what Del was saying heard that. He turned away from the huddle, disgusted at what he just heard. He said to himself, "Are you kidding me? He's telling him to be selfish. All he ever does is tell me I'm selfish and need to be unselfish. And he's telling Rem to be selfish. What a crock!"

Del finished with his instructions and the huddle broke. The Wolves and Hawks headed out to the floor. The next eight minutes would determine which team would be heading to the state tournament and which would be going home. The Wolves' ultimate goal of getting to the state tournament would all come down to this quarter.

For the first two minutes of the quarter, both teams played well. The defense for both was solid, but the offense was better. Remington saw why Del had said what he said. Because he had been so focused on setting his teammates up so much in the first three quarters, the Hawks were laying off of him a bit. By the end of the third quarter, Remington already had 11 assists in the game, but he had only scored 6 points. He picked up his 12th assist a minute into the fourth quarter, on a nice one-hand bounce pass to Nick on a backdoor cut.

The next time down, though, Remington caught it on the left wing, and started to swing the ball to Billy Thompson in the corner to his left. Gallatin was playing a zone defense, and the man in front of him bit on the fake, and started moving toward Billy in the corner. By the time he recognized the fake, Remington had shot an open three-pointer—nothing but net.

On the next possession, Remington caught it in the same spot. He did the same ball fake to Billy in the left corner, but this time the defender stayed home—exactly what Remington figured would happen. He followed the pass fake up by starting into his shot motion, and the defender elevated to block the shot. However, Remington pulled the ball back down, swept it across his body into a right-handed dribble, and drove into the lane. Out of his left eye, he saw Billy cutting from the corner behind the zone towards the basket. Remington looked at Nick on the opposite wing and elevated as if to pass to him. Instead he fired a short, bullet pass across his body to his left as Billy was stepping into the lane. The middle defender had already been stepping toward Nick, assuming Remington was throwing it to him. Billy caught the pass and laid it in the basket. With Remington's 13th assist of the game, the Wolves were up by 5.

Cade continued to sit on the bench. The longer he sat, the more upset he got. "How can Coach do this to me? I'm the best player. I need to be on the floor. My team needs me on the floor. They need me to score. This sucks. I can't do anything here on the bench."

He could take it no more. He walked down towards the coaches, told Bruce to move one seat down, and sat down next to Coach Larson. He leaned forward to speak across the two assistants to Del, who was seated on the end of the bench. "Coach. Put me in! I need to be out there. They need me out there."

Chapter 22

Del looked at him. "Seriously, Cade? They need you out there? Have you been watching the game? It seems like they're doing fine without you. In fact, I'd go so far as to say they're doing better without you."

Cade blurted out, "Why do you hate me so much?"

Del looked at him and thought for split-second that he couldn't believe this was happening at this moment. He said to Braden, "Coach, switch seats with me." As he got up to switch seats with Braden, he said to Kevin, "Take care of things on the floor for a minute, will you?"

He sat down next to Cade and said, "First of all, this is not the time for this. If you haven't noticed I'm trying to coach a playoff basketball game to make it to the state tournament, and we have five minutes left to go. I'm a bit pre-occupied and busy, so I'm going to make this real quick. I don't hate you, Cade. I like you a lot, always have. It's your attitude that I hate. You've got passion and skill, and that can be a great combination when it's directed the right way, for the good of others, for the good of your team. But you direct it in the wrong way. You use those only for yourself. You care nothing about anyone else on your team. That's what I hate. Any other questions that can't wait until after the game?"

"Am I going to get to play again?" asked Cade.

"I don't know," said Del. "I'd ask if you're going to play like a team player and do the things that have been asked of you all year long, but I know you'll say 'yes.' But then all year long you've just gone out and done your own thing, not a team thing. I can't have that anymore. Your teammates are busting their butts out there, playing together, and doing everything we've asked of them. You refuse to do that. I can't trust you anymore."

"Coach, I swear if you put me in, I'll be a team player. I won't shoot it. I'll only pass it."

"That's not what I want, Cade. That's foolish to say. You're a good shooter, so we want you to shoot it. But we want you to shoot it within the flow of the offense and when you're open for a good shot. We don't want you forcing up shots. We want you playing with your teammates not against them."

"I will, Coach. Please give me one more chance."

"All right. I'll think about it."

Del turned and looked back out on the floor just as a Gallatin player was intercepting a pass and taking it down court for a layup that tied the game. The scoreboard clock showed 4:17 left in the game.

Del turned back to Cade. "All right, Cade. Here's your chance. You've got four minutes to be a team player. Four minutes to decide if we're going to fulfill our goal of going to the state tournament together or if you're going to play by yourself and have tonight be the end of it all. Make the right choice, Cade. Go for Mike."

Cade hopped off the bench and reported to the scorer's table as Del stood up and called for a timeout. As the team came off the floor, Cade met Mike, high-fived him, and told him "Mike, I'm in for you." Nick, Tim, and Remington looked at each other and rolled their eyes.

In the timeout, Del outlined both the defensive and offensive game plans. He alerted everyone again that with Cade back on the floor be ready for Trout to be up tight on him or laying off of him. He told Cade not to force action that wasn't there, to find his teammates. Cade nodded his head, but nobody believed he was listening.

The first play out of the timeout saw Remington with the ball on the point. He started to drive towards Cade's side of the floor. He wanted to see how Aaron Trout was playing Cade. Trout slid off of Cade to help on Remington's drive. Remington dished it to Cade, who was open for a split-second before Trout recovered onto him. Rather than forcing up a shot, Cade quickly surveyed his options. He took one dribble to his left, and Remington's man jumped off of Remington to double-team Cade. Cade saw Remington open out of the corner of his eye, and threw a nice bounce pass between Trout and Remington's defender. Remington caught it and laid it in the basket. Remington pointed at Cade and yelled, "Nice pass, Cade!" as the Sacajawea crowd went wild. Cade pointed back at Remington as he took his place on the press.

Unfortunately, Gallatin entered the ball quickly and Billy had not gotten to his position on the press yet. One of the Gallatin forwards recognized that and sprinted to the open area. The Gallatin guard looked ahead and passed it to one of his teammates. Now Brian Johnson had to come out, which left the basket open. The Gallatin forward tossed a pass toward the rim, and his teammate caught it in mid-air and laid it in to tie the game back up.

Chapter 22

The Wolves' next possession saw Cade start on an attack from the wing but get cut off. He kicked it out to Remington who swung it to Nick. Nick did not have an opening, so he passed it back to Remington, and Remington set up the offense. Gallatin's defense stiffened, and each time the Wolves thought they had an open drive to the basket, it was shut down. With a little over three minutes left in the game, Remington sent a pass to Brian on the wing. As Brian caught it and turned, he lost his footing and took an extra step to recover from his slip. The referee blew the whistle and signaled a traveling violation. Gallatin's ball.

Once again, the Wolves set up their press. Gallatin inbounded the ball, and their point guard tried to beat Nick up the side of the floor. As he turned the corner on Nick, Cade was there to apply the trap. The guard elevated to make the pass, but with cat-quick hands, Cade stripped the ball from him and grabbed it. He spotted Billy cutting to the middle of the floor, and Cade hit him on his cut. Billy caught the ball, found Remington streaking toward the basket, and hit him for the layup. With 2:48 left, the Wolves were up by two.

Gallatin took possession of the ball and this time they beat the Wolves press. However, Brian Johnson was back and did not allow an easy layup, and Gallatin pulled the ball out to set up their offense. They were patient with the ball, and the Wolves were very focused defensively. Gallatin could not get past the Wolves or get an open look, but the Wolves could not get a steal or a turnover.

Gallatin had the ball for twenty seconds before Aaron Trout received a pass on the right wing with Billy Thompson guarding him. Trout shot-faked and started his drive around Billy. Cade was one man away, and he quickly slid away from his man toward Trout. He positioned himself perfectly in Trout's path, planted his feet, and absorbed Trout's hit. Cade fell to the floor as the official blew his whistle and motioned a charging foul on Trout. From the floor, Cade yelled "Yeah!" and his teammates ran to him to help him up.

"Nice job, Cade! Way to take the charge!" They high-fived him and got set up in their press break. Cade was smiling.

Del looked at Kevin and said, "Haven't seen that in a while."

Kevin said, "Cade taking a charge?"

Del said, "Well, yeah that, too. But I meant Cade smiling with his teammates."

Kevin nodded, "Yeah, you're right. It's nice to see. Let's hope we continue to see it for the next three minutes."

The Wolves inbounded the ball against Gallatin's press. Unfortunately, they could not get the ball to Remington in the middle of the floor. Gallatin's coach had put Trout in the middle of the press and told him not to leave Remington. Nick had the ball and was trapped in the corner. He saw Brian at the half-court line and threw an overhead pass to him. However, a Gallatin defender also saw that developing and drifted towards Brian. Nick's pass was tipped by one of the players in the trap, and the Gallatin defender headed towards Brian and picked it off. As he caught it, he turned towards the basket and saw one of his teammates on the opposite side of the court stepping towards the 3-point line with nobody on him. He rifled a bullet pass to his teammate. His teammate caught it in rhythm and stepped into an open 3-pointer, and the ball swished through the net. Gallatin was up by 1 with just over 2:00 left to play.

Gallatin went into their press again, but this time, Remington inbounded the ball. As Nick caught it in the corner. Remington stepped onto the floor and with Trout in the middle of the floor where his coach told him to be, Remington was open in the free throw lane. Nick sent the ball right back to him before the Trout got up on him. As was so often the case, once the ball was in Remington's hands, the press was all but broken. Remington started his attack dribble up the floor. As Trout came up and reached for the ball, Remington dribbled the ball behind his back from his right hand to his left. Trout went flying past him. Remington dribbled the ball back across his body to his right and found Cade up ahead on the right side of the floor.

As he looked at Cade and started to pick up his dribble, the last man on the press stepped out towards Cade. As that was happening, Brian Johnson was sprinting down the left side of the lane. Remington fired a pass to Cade. The Gallatin defender continued to step towards Cade. In one quick motion, Cade caught the ball, turned, and tossed it up towards the front of the rim. Brian caught the ball at its peak with both hands, and slammed it through the hoop, a perfect alley-oop dunk. The crowd erupted, as did the players on the floor and on the bench. Brian immediately sprinted towards Cade.

"Nice pass, Cade!" he yelled.

"Sweet dunk, Bri!" Cade yelled back.

Chapter 22

Gallatin looked stunned. They were now down by 1 with under two minutes remaining. Their coach called a timeout.

The Wolves were all high-fiving each other, but especially Brian and Cade as they came off the floor. Del grabbed Cade before he got to the bench. "That's how you play team ball, Cade. Great job! Keep it up!" Cade smiled, nodded, and sat down.

Del said, "All right, nice job. We need to stay focused. We need to continue to defend them tough, and we need to continue to play together on the offensive end. We're going to drop to straight man-to-man this possession. You need to be aware of their dribble-drives and kick outs for three. Help on drives, but then help the helpers and challenge shooters. On offense we're going to spread it out. This is not an "ice it, hold for one shot" spread. This is a spread to score. You've run this many times this year. You're making them come get you, but you're also looking to attack. The more they scramble to get you, the more your teammates will be open. Take any good, open look that you get, but don't force anything up, especially in traffic. Get it?"

All five guys said, "Got it." They stepped out of the huddle onto the floor. Remington picked up their point guard as he came across the half-line. There was now 1:45 left in the game. Gallatin ran a play with a double-screen for their best shooter, but the Wolves switched the screen. Gallatin couldn't get the shot off, so they re-set their offense with 1:35 left.

The Gallatin point guard called another play. A big post player came up towards the point and set a screen for the point guard. On the pick and roll, Gallatin had a man spotted up in each corner. Billy was guarding a man in the opposite corner from the side of the floor that the point guard dribbled to. The point guard saw Billy was off of his man ready to help in the lane. The point guard faked the bounce pass to the rolling big man and fired an overhead pass to his teammate in the corner. By the time Billy figured that out, it was too late. He had ranged a little too far away from the shooter, leaving him open for a little too long. His man caught the pass, and in one fluid motion launched a 3-pointer that swished through the net. The Gallatin fans erupted, and Gallatin now had a 2-point lead with 1:20 to go.

Remington received the inbounds pass in the backcourt and was immediately trapped. He found Cade cutting to the middle of the floor. Cade caught Remington's pass and attacked. He was dribbling hard up the middle of the floor, with one man back for Gallatin and one chasing him down from the right side. He peeled his dribble back out to the left sideline to set up the spread offense. He passed it to Remington who set them up in the offense. Remington was out at the half-line, with Nick to his right and Cade to his left. Billy and Brian were down in the corners. The Gallatin players were laying off of them since Gallatin now had the lead.

The clock read 1:07, and Del realized that his spread offense would not work because Gallatin did not have to come out and defend the Wolves closely since Gallatin had the lead. If the Wolves wanted to hold the ball, time would run out on them. Del stood up, yelled out, "Set it up. Run 2!" This was the play they had run earlier when Cade decided to do his own thing instead of pass it to a wide-open Brian. Del hoped this time Cade would run it right.

The players moved to their spots to run the play. Like the last time they ran it, the first pass went to Cade. Brian set his back screen for Remington and then was reading whether or not to roll to the basket or pop to the three-point line. His defender sensed that this was the same play as earlier in the quarter, and he stayed tight on Brian, not letting him step to the 3-point line. Remington continued through the lane after his pass, but Cade could not get him the ball. However, Brian read that his man was overplaying him out at the 3-point line. Brian took one more step out as if he were wanting to get to the 3-point line. His man jumped out hard on him. Brian planted his outside foot and then cut towards the basket. Cade faked his pass to the 3-point line to freeze the defender for a split-second, and Brian was now open cutting to the basket. Cade passed it to him, but Remington's man slid over to help on Brian. Brian saw that, and he saw Remington open under the basket. He tossed a soft pass up towards the rim, and Remington caught it and laid it in the basket to tie the game up with :50 to go. The Wolves fans erupted as the Gallatin coach signaled to the referees for a timeout.

The Wolves were high-fiving each other as they came to the bench. Remington said, "Great pass, Bri! Way to find him, Cade!" Cade smiled and said, "Way to finish, Rem."

Del stepped into the huddle and said, "All right. We need to buckle down this possession. Since we are tied, they may just try to hold it for the last shot. Fifty seconds is a long time to hold it, though, especially against good, quick guards like we have. They are in the bonus, so we don't want to foul them. However, we can't give them any easy, open looks. Keep them in front of you, switch all screens, and challenge all jumpers. Don't run past them at the 3-point line, though. On any shot attempt, we all—and that means guys on the bench, too—need to yell, 'Shot!' That is your clue to get a block out. Stay aggressive, but don't foul them.

"Depending on the situation when we get the ball back, if you have a wide-open attack off of a steal up high, go take it to the rack. Otherwise, I will call timeout to set up what we want to run, so we make sure we get the look we need. Any questions?"

The boys all shook their heads "No," and Del said, "One more thing. Trust each other. Trust your buddy next to you. Trust your training. Trust what you have done all year long to prepare for this moment. We were built for this. Now let's go out and take this thing!" The Wolves all jumped up off the bench screaming. They put their hands in the huddle, as Nick yelled, "Wolves on 3... 1, 2, 3," and they all yelled, "WOLVES!"

As Del expected, Gallatin came out and attempted to hold the ball in their own version of a spread offense. They employed more of a 4-corners approach, putting their two guards out high and wide near half-court, two forwards in the corners, and their big man in the middle at the free throw line. The goal was to keep the ball in the hands of the two guards until they were ready to run a play, probably with around 10 seconds left, Del figured. The forwards and the center would be used only as pressure releases if the guards got in trouble with the ball.

Remington and Nick were guarding the two guards, Cade and Billy had the forwards in the corners, and Brian had the big man in the middle. For the first fifteen seconds of the possession, Gallatin's guards kept the ball, forcing Remington and Nick to chase them. The big man set screens for the guard without the ball to get him open. Their plan was working well.

With :32 left, Nick tried to anticipate his own man's cut from the 3-point line towards the half-line, and he jumped up into the passing lane. However, Nick's man read his mind. He faked like he was popping out there, planted his foot and cut back door. Remington's man had the ball and saw this whole thing developing. He couldn't believe their good fortune. He was going to make a pass to a wide-open teammate 12 feet from the basket. All his teammate would need to do was catch the ball, take one dribble, and lay it in the basket for the lead.

What Remington's man didn't see was Cade sneaking over from guarding his man in the opposite corner towards Nick's man. Remington's man could not see Cade because Brian and the man he was guarding by the free-throw line blocked his view. He had already been sagging off of his man towards the lane when he saw Nick's man back cut to get open. As the point guard started to pick the ball up to throw the pass to the cutter heading to the basket, Cade stepped right where the man was cutting.

As Remington's man began to throw his pass, Remington put his hands up, making him throw the ball a little higher and a little softer than he wanted to. This trajectory gave Cade the extra split-second he needed, and he stepped across the lane towards the ball in mid-air. Cade stepped underneath Nick's man, whose arms were reaching up to grab the ball. In one swift move, Cade stepped under him and vaulted himself up into the air, snatching the ball right out of the air, just before it reached the Gallatin player's fingertips. Cade came down with the ball with a powerful jump stop, and held it tight to his chest. Del jumped off the bench and yelled "Timeout!" There were twenty-seven seconds left in the game.

The boys came to the bench slapping Cade on the back and yelling. Remington said, "Great job, Cade!" They high-fived each other and sat down on the bench.

Del drew up and explained what he wanted them to do. They would spread the floor and hold the ball for one shot. This time it was a spread to hold it for a final shot. He told them to start their play with eight seconds left. He did not want to give Gallatin any time to score if the Wolves did not score. He wanted the shot to go up with less than three seconds left.

Del drew up a play they had practiced all year but had never run in a game. He wanted to save it for a moment when they might need it. It would be something their opponent had never seen in person or on film. But first they needed to spread the floor to hold the ball. Del told them, "Take care of the ball. If we don't get a shot off, we can go into overtime and win this thing. But if we lose the ball, then we give them a chance to win it. Value that ball!"

As they stood up to go out to the floor, Del huddled them all up and said, "Boys, I believe in you, I know you believe in yourselves! Now believe in each other. If you do that, we're going to win this game right now!" Nick yelled out "Wolves on 3... 1, 2, 3," and they all yelled, "WOLVES!"

Chapter 22

They set up their sideline out of bounds play, and Billy entered it to Remington in the back court. Much to Remington's delight, the man guarding him was laying off of him waiting at the 3-point line. All of Gallatin's defenders were packed in instead of being out with their men in the four corners. Their coach did not want to go out and guard them out high and give up a backdoor layup, so they were going to let the Wolves hold it for the last shot.

Just like Del diagrammed and explained in the timeout, with the clock reading 0:12, Remington took the ball to the point and called out "Set it up." Cade went to the right corner, and Nick and Brian set themselves up just outside the free-throw line on Cade's side of the floor. Billy went down to the left-side of the lane near the basket. At the :08 mark, Remington yelled out "Go!" Billy popped out to the left wing. Billy's man was worried about giving up the back door, so he played behind Billy, allowing him to catch the ball on the wing at the 3-point line. Remington followed his pass for a hand-off from Billy. While the ball was in flight, Nick and Brian took two steps towards the middle of the free throw lane from the opposite side of it from where Remington was receiving a hand-off from Billy. They were merely decoying what their real plan was.

After receiving the ball from Billy, Remington turned and faced the basket. Billy then turned and screened for him to take his dribble back to the middle towards the free-throw line. After his pick, Billy was supposed to pop back out towards the wing. This would free up some room for Remington on his drive. However, the play was not designed for Billy to receive the ball. It was actually set up to go to the other side of the floor. After the hand-off occurred, Nick and Brian turned around, left the lane, and went to set a double screen for Cade coming from the far corner on the other side of the floor. The two of them were just outside the lane, standing shoulder to shoulder with their backs facing the free-throw line. Nick was closer to the basket and Brian was to the outside of him. Cade took two steps towards the basket and then came up hard off their screen. He was supposed to read what his defender did and do one of three things: curl around the screen into the lane and cut to the basket, pop out towards the 3-point line at the wing, or fade right back to the corner from which he came.

As Remington started his dribble towards the lane, Cade came off the screen. His man had started to go under Nick and Brian's screen, so Cade stepped out towards the 3-point line on the right wing. His man quickly read that Cade was doing that, so he started to run back up to the wing to chase Cade out to the 3-point line. However, Brian's man also saw that Cade was getting open at the 3-point line. Brian's man stepped out in the passing lane towards Cade to take away Remington's pass to Cade.

That meant that both Cade's and Brian's defenders were now stepping out to guard Cade at the 3-point line. That left only Nick's man to guard Nick and Brian. Nick's man was standing in the free-throw lane between Nick and Remington. He was ready to help stop any dribble penetration into the lane. As Remington came off of Billy's screen, his defender and Billy's defender got caught up for a split-second. This gave Remington the small space he needed to get one more dribble into the lane. As he did this, Nick's man took one step into the middle of the lane towards Remington. Nick turned towards his man and stepped up behind him to screen him. If he put his body right on the man's back it would be a foul, so he stayed about a foot or two off of him.

With Brian's and Cade's men both stepping out to guard Cade at the 3-point line and Nick's man being screened by Nick in the lane, there was nobody to guard Brian. Brian rolled right behind Nick and stepped towards the basket. As Nick's defender realized what was happening, he immediately turned around to try to get to Brian. However, Nick was right there setting the screen on him.

Remington's eyes widened as he saw the play developing exactly as Coach had drawn it up and they had practiced it all year. It just never worked this way in practice because the defenders knew what was coming. With three seconds left on the clock, Remington tossed a soft pass up towards the rim. Brian caught the ball and in one fell swoop jammed it through. The Wolves were now up by two, and the Sacajawea crowd was going crazy!

Gallatin was out of timeouts. The Gallatin defender being screened by Nick tried to run to pick the ball up off the floor and get out of bounds to throw it in. By the time he got around Nick's body and to the ball and stepped out of bounds to throw it in, the buzzer went off. The Wolves had won the game!

Gallatin's players slumped to the floor. The Wolves fans exploded in cheers. The Wolves' entire bench ran onto the court hugging one another and finding anyone they could to hug. Del, Kevin, and Braden all turned to each other and did a group hug while jumping up and down, yelling, "We did it!" After the buzzer sounded, Brian had immediately turned to Nick and bear-hugged him. Billy ran to the both of them and tried hugging them both at the same time.

Remington turned towards Cade and ran straight at him. Cade was grinning ear-to-ear as he put his arms out wide, ready to take Remington's hug from him. As they embraced, Cade yelled to Remington, "WE DID IT! We're going to State!" Remington let out a long, loud, "YEEAAAAHHHHH!" as he and Cade hugged.

A moment later they were both mobbed by their teammates. The fans poured out onto the floor. The Wolves had finally beaten their archrivals and were headed to the state tournament. Players and fans alike felt such a rush of jubilation, and they were letting it all out. Security quickly came out on the floor and ushered the fans back to the bleachers.

Ideas to Consider:
- **How did Cade grow as a player by the end of this game?**
- **How did Coach Brooks grow as a coach by the end of this game?**

Chapter 23

As the security people were dealing with the fans, Del, Kevin, and Braden made their way out to the floor to grab the players and get them into the handshake line. While the joyous celebration was a great reward for all that they had accomplished, Del also wanted them to show class and get into the handshake line that the Gallatin players were waiting for. Del knew all too well what the players and coaches of Gallatin were feeling. As he grabbed the boys into a circle amidst all the noise and chaos, he yelled out to them, "Boys, show class in the handshake line. You know what they are going through. Stay humble!"

The players and coaches made their way through the line. As Del had taught them and reinforced with them throughout the year, they looked each player in the eye, shook hands or high-fived them, and said, "Nice game." The Gallatin players looked shell-shocked, many of them with tears in their eyes. The Wolves completely understood why.

The Wolves felt a mixture of empathy, redemption, and joy as they made their way through the line. They were empathetic because they knew how much the Gallatin players were hurting. They felt redemption, though, because Gallatin was their archrival, and they had beaten the Wolves twice this year. They had also knocked the Wolves out of the tournament in other years in the past. But most of all, the Wolves felt absolute joy. However, they stayed humble and did not laugh and joke with each other while going through the line.

After the handshakes came a quick trophy presentation. This was the first hardware the Wolves were taking home in Del's time as their coach. He felt a personal sense of satisfaction and relief that it had finally happened. The boys felt extreme joy and jubilation as the PA announcer congratulated the Wolves on their victory and the tournament director handed Del the 3rd-place trophy. Del raised it in the air towards the Sacajawea crowd and they erupted in cheers. He then turned and handed it to the first player he

Chapter 23

saw next to him—Cade. Cade hoisted it in the air with the biggest grin on his face that anyone could remember seeing on him. The crowd erupted again. There were a few photos snapped, and then the boys had to exit the floor, as the next game's teams were already warming up.

The boys headed into the locker room. Del was stopped by a reporter, and he did a quick two-minute interview. As he opened the door of the locker room and the boys saw him, they exploded with the loudest yell in a locker room he had ever heard. They began jumping around, high-fiving each other, and yelling, "On to State! On to State!" echoing their crowd's chant in the bleachers moments ago. Del joined in the chant for a few seconds, and then put his hands up to get them to quiet down.

"Congratulations, boys," he said. "I've been waiting a long time to say this to you." He paused and then yelled out, "You're going to the state tournament!" They erupted again with cheers and whoops.

Del continued. "Like I reminded you before the game, at the beginning of the year we set one win-loss goal for the season." He turned toward the board and pointed at the words as he said, "GET TO STATE." He paused as he looked back at all the smiling faces in front of him.

Del continued. "But we also put an even more important word up there on the board." He turned back to the board and pointed at the word.

Before he could get the word out, the entire team yelled out, "TOGETHER!"

Del continued, "Well, that's exactly what we did tonight. I couldn't be prouder of all of you. It took a great team effort to beat a really good team. There were so many big plays and so many key moments. Remington's leadership and ability to find people was a huge key."

Del looked down at the stat-sheet that he was handed by the tournament scorekeeper as he headed into the locker room. He searched for one stat, found it, and said, "Yep. That's what I thought. Rem, I don't know if it's a Divisional record for assists, Buddy, but you had 14 of them today!" The team erupted again, slapping Remington on the back and rubbing his head.

Del continued. "Brian, Billy, Nick, Tim, Bruce, Mike, everyone—you guys all came up big in so many moments. So many key stops, scores, and times where you found each other." Del had purposefully left Cade off the list. Cade dropped his head, crushed that Del had not mentioned him. Del was waiting to see Cade's reaction, and as soon as he saw it, he continued.

"This was truly a team effort. But the team effort I'm most proud of and most excited about tonight was Cade's." Cade looked up from the floor, with tears in his eyes. His teammates started chanting, "Cade! Cade! Cade!" Cade smiled, absorbing the admiration of his teammates.

Del said, "Cade, that last four minutes was some of the best basketball I've ever seen you play. Your impact on this game and on your team was the greatest I've ever seen from you. And you know what? You did it all without taking one shot from the field. You put your own individual ego aside, put your team first, made all the right decisions and all the right plays, and we're going to the state tournament because of it. I couldn't be happier for you and prouder of you. Great job, Cade. You keep playing that way, and I like our chances next week at the state tournament." Cade's teammates started chanting his name again.

As the chant started to die down, Remington raised his hand and said, "Coach, can I say something?"

Del said, "Absolutely."

Remington turned to Cade and said, "When the game ended and I ran up to you, you said, 'We did it!' You're absolutely right, Cade. WE did it. All of us, and you were huge down the stretch. I may have had 14 assists, but your assists in the last four minutes were by far the biggest we've had all season. We needed every one of those from you and you delivered. But your biggest play of the night may have been one where you didn't even touch the ball. It was your cut on the last play. Brian wouldn't have been so open if you hadn't made the perfect cut off of his and Nick's screen. You sold that thing so well, both those guys went with you. Gallatin was so worried about you getting an open jump shot that they left Brian open for dunk! Can you believe that? You were the key, Cade. And now we're going to state because of it. It was so awesome playing with you like you played tonight, Cade."

Cade, sitting two seats away from Remington, smiled and said, "Thanks, Rem."

The players all clapped and cheered and echoed Remington's words. Cade smiled stood up, stepped out to the front of the room, and faced them. "Guys, I've got to say this in front of all of you. Rem, you're wrong." He paused, gathered his thoughts and said, "You were the key. You've been the key this whole year. You're the ultimate team player ever, and we needed you more than anybody else on this team. Nick was right last week. I've had my head so far up my ass I couldn't see what I was doing. I was so worried about me getting mine and worried that you were getting what I wanted, that I just never saw it. But now I do. This is so much more fun playing this way. I just want to say to all of you I'm sorry it took me so long to figure it out. Sorry I've been so hard to play with."

Cade paused as some of the players responded with comments like, "Hey, don't worry about it, man." But he put his hand up and said, "Please let me finish. Rem, I'm most sorry for how I treated you, how much of a jerk I was to you. I guess I was jealous that you were getting the recognition you were getting. I was mad that it wasn't me getting all that."

Cade had tears welling up in his eyes as he continued. "But now I see it. You deserved it more than me. You're the greatest team player I've ever seen, and I've been wasting my time playing with you and not appreciating it. Well, that ends today. Thanks for all you've done to help me be a better player and for all you've done to help this team be the best it can be."

Remington didn't know what to say. He, too, had tears in his eyes as he listened to Cade. There was an awkward split-second where he didn't know what to say. He then said, "Don't worry about it, dude. I knew what you were going through. I knew how badly you wanted to be the man, but I also knew how badly you wanted to win. I just wanted to help you get both of those things, man. But ultimately, we're a team." Remington stood up facing Cade, but he turned towards the whole team as he spoke. "We win together, we lose together, and we learn together. That's what this whole year has been about for all of us." He turned back to Cade, "And now you know it, too, Cade. Now you know how much fun this whole team thing is. There ain't nothing like this feeling, is there?"

Cade nodded his head and said, "Nope. I never felt anything like this. This is the greatest feeling I've ever felt."

Remington responded, "Absolutely, Bro. And look where we are now." Remington raised his voice as he said, "WE'RE GOING TO STATE!" They both smiled huge smiles, and Remington reached out and hugged Cade and Cade hugged him back like he had never hugged anyone in his life. The entire team jumped up off the locker room benches and all started jumping around Remington and Cade and yelled, "ON TO STATE! ON TO STATE! ON TO STATE!"

After the boys' chanting died down, Del quieted them down again and said, "All right, boys. We've got the rest of the day today and a day tomorrow to enjoy this, get rested, and then get to work on Monday to prepare for state. I want you to go out and thank your families, friends, and fans, and celebrate with them for a few minutes. Then get back in here and get showered."

Ideas to Consider:

- What changed for Cade? What made him figure it out?
- Why do some athletes like Cade behave the way they do? Some of them never figure out the value of "team." What can coaches and teammates do to try to get them to see the value in being a great team player? When in a young athlete's life should this messaging start?

Chapter 24

The boys and coaches all filed out of the locker room. After about five minutes, Del went back into the locker room and sat down, thinking about all that happened up to that point. Like any season, there were so many ups and downs that the team went through this year. He thought about all the things he was glad he did and all the things he wished he would have done differently. Of course, Cade was at the top of that list.

This year was a learning experience for Del. He knew he should have handled Cade differently, holding him accountable for his actions more. The players on the team were the ones who taught Del that. He was so glad that they achieved their goal of making it to the state tournament because it meant that they all got to spend another week together. He was also glad that Cade finally seemed to come around in the last few minutes of the game tonight. He hoped it would be a turning point for Cade, not just for the state tournament, but also for if he played in college.

As Del sat there with his thoughts, Cade came back into the locker room after going out to visit with family and friends. Del called him over and Cade sat down next to Del. Del said, "I'm proud of you, Cade." Cade looked up at him and Del continued. "Proud of the way you played the last four minutes and proud of what you did here in the locker room a few minutes ago. That was a huge step for you, and it was huge for your teammates to hear that from you."

Cade said, "Thanks, Coach."

Del said, "My only question is, 'Do you really feel that way?' Do you really feel like the best feeling in the world is playing with your teammates that way, not just playing on your own and them just happening to be on the same court as you? Or were you just saying that?"

"No, Coach. I meant every word I said. It feels awesome."

"Cade, there is nothing you will ever feel like the feeling you get sharing great moments like this with teammates. Nothing! No individual accomplishments, no stats, no personal glory. Nothing can take the place of the feeling you're feeling right now—sharing a great moment like this with your teammates. Once you get addicted to that feeling, you gotta' have it all the time. And once you get to that point, you start to become the best you can be."

Cade struggled to find the right words. Finally, he said, "I see it now, Coach. I also know this: I want more of this feeling."

Del smiled and said, "Well, now you know how to get it. The question is will you keep doing what you need to do to get it."

As Cade started to raise his head to answer, Del put up his hand as if to say "Stop" and cut him off by saying, "Wait. Don't say anything. You know why?"

Cade shook his head, "No."

"Because your words won't provide the answer to this question. The only things that can provide that answer are your actions and time. We will see the answer in how you play next week, not what you say." Del paused. "We'll also see it when you're playing in college."

Cade looked up at him and said, "I don't know if I'm going to play in college, Coach."

Del said, "Really? Why not?"

"Because I still haven't been recruited by anyone, and it's so late in the season. I just want a shot at it. I don't need a guarantee. I just want a chance. I realize now that I probably blew it with the way I played last year and most of this year. I wish I would have listened to you before the last four minutes tonight. I had so much fun playing that way with the guys. Now that I know how that feels, I want to keep doing that. I can't wait to play that way next week at State. And I just want to have a chance to play that way in college."

Del smiled and said, "I knew that you'd feel that way once you truly bought into being a team player and saw the results. I knew it would have that kind of impact on you, while at the same time you having the kind of impact you had on your team tonight."

Chapter 24

He paused, then said. "Cade, I'm not the only coach who knew that about you. There are three college coaches out there right now who just watched you play. I talked to them yesterday about you. I told them the truth, that you were struggling with the team game, but that if you got a taste of it, look out. I knew they would be here today, so I asked them to watch you. For the first three quarters, I don't imagine they were all that impressed by what they saw. But after the way you played at the end today, they saw what I knew you had in you. They saw what they wanted in a player in their programs—someone with the skills to handle the college game, but also someone who understands the value and importance of team." Del paused then said, "Cade, this might be the chance you were asking for. They're outside in the bleachers waiting to talk to you and to Rem."

Cade smiled and said, "Really? What schools are here, Coach?"

"Two of them are schools that had already contacted you—Rocky and Tech."

Cade smiled and said, "Cool. I like both of those schools. I was already accepted to each of them. I could see myself playing at either one." He paused then asked, "Who's the other one?"

Del smiled, and then said, "Oh just a little school in the western part of the state called the University of Montana."

Cade looked shocked. He said, "You mean the Grizzlies want to talk to me!?"

"Yep," said Del with a big grin. "U of M. D1, Baby. Their head coach and one of his assistants are here. The assistant stopped me after we all went back out to our families and asked if they could talk to you. I talked with him for a couple of minutes."

Cade grinned. He was stunned. He had only scored nine points the entire game. How could the University of Montana be interested in him?

Del had an idea he knew what Cade was thinking. "It was pretty eye-opening listening to him. He said that he and Coach Baker saw what you were made of in the last four minutes today. They saw a player who could have a major impact on their team by being a great teammate. They already knew you had the skills, knew you could score from the film of a couple of games I sent them a few weeks ago. Coach Baker was interested in you immediately after they watched that film, but they didn't know if you had the right attitude to play for them. They didn't know if you were team-oriented enough. And quite honestly, they didn't like what they saw earlier in today's game. But he said they were impressed with how you handled those last four minutes, and they want to talk to you."

Cade's stomach was churning and his nerves were jumping. Del continued, "Now, this doesn't mean that they're going to offer you a scholarship, Cade. It means that they saw a team player out there today, one who they are interested in." Del paused and said, "Cade, I think that chance that you were saying you want is waiting outside those doors. All three of them are good opportunities for you. Hustle up, get a quick shower, and get dressed and go out and talk to them, and listen to what they have to say. I will go tell them you'll be out in a few minutes."

As Del started toward the door to go talk to the coaches, Cade stood up and said, "Coach." Del turned around and saw that Cade had tears in his eyes. Cade walked over to Del put his arms around him, hugged him, and buried his head in Del's shoulder. "Thanks, Coach."

Del was taken aback. He'd never seen emotion like this toward him from Cade. Cade continued speaking through the tears. "Thanks for not giving up on me. I'm so sorry I acted the way I did. I didn't deserve to be in there at the end. I probably didn't deserve to be on this team for a long time now. But you never gave up on me. You stuck with me. Thank you so much for not giving up on me."

Cade cried into Del's shoulder, and Del held onto him. "I couldn't give up on you, Cade. I always knew you had it in you. But I also figured you would have to learn your lesson before you could get to this point. I'm so proud of you, Cade. So proud of the young man you've become and will continue to grow to be."

Cade pulled his head off of Del's shoulder, pulled away from Del and said, "Thanks, Coach." He wiped the tears from his eyes and said, "I couldn't have done any of it without you."

"You're welcome, Cade. Now go get showered, while I go talk to these coaches."

Chapter 24

Ideas to Consider:
- **What has Cade's dream been for a long time?**
- **What happened that has led to his dream possibly coming true?**

Chapter 25

When Del walked out the locker room door, he came through a tunnel that headed towards the court. The two teams that were about to play in the next game were finishing their warm ups. As Del turned the corner at the end of the tunnel, he saw the Rocky coach, Jim White, and the Tech coach, Rich Jenkins, talking to each other. A little further past them, he saw the University of Montana head coach, Pat Baker and his assistant Travis Lake, talking with Remington.

Del stopped to tell the coaches that Cade would be out in a couple of minutes. They said, "Okay." Then the Rich Jenkins said, "Well, it looks like we don't have a shot at the Roberts kid."

Del said, "Why not?"

Jim White said, "Do you see who he's talking to right now? If the U wants him already, it doesn't look good for us." Rich Jenkins nodded his head in agreement.

Del said, "Well, things can change, right? They might not stay all that interested in him. Or he might not be all that interested in them."

Rich Jenkins looked at Del with a funny look on his face. "Okay, two things. First of all, what kid is NOT going to be interested in playing D1 if a D1 school is interested in him? Second, there's no way they are going to lose interest in him. That kid is the real deal. He has everything that a coach is looking for. He can shoot it, handle it, defend, and he's the best passer I've seen in the last 10 years."

Coach White had nodded at everything Coach Jenkins was saying, and he added, "And he seems to be the ultimate team player. He always has his head up. He knows where everyone should be, gets them there, and then puts the ball in the right spots when they get there. He's always picking his teammates up. He's totally focused on you in huddles. He's cheering on his teammates when he's on the bench. That kid is something special. I'm afraid he's too special for us to be able to get him."

Del was listening to everything the two coaches were saying. His smile grew bigger and bigger with each comment. He then said, "Yeah. I can't argue with anything you said. He's the best I've ever coached and maybe ever seen. His skills are solid, but it's the entire package that makes him so special. And you know what the best part of it is?"

The two coaches both said, "What?" at the same time.

Del smiled and said, "I get him for another week and then a whole other year!"

The two coaches laughed, and Jim White said, "Yeah, well don't screw him up!"

All three of them laughed together. Del turned and Cade was coming out of the locker room door. As he got up to them, Del said, "Jeez that's the fastest you've ever showered."

Nodding toward the coaches, Cade said, "I didn't want to keep them waiting."

Del introduced him to both coaches. "Cade, this is Coach Jenkins from Montana Tech and Coach White from Rocky Mountain College." Cade shook both the coaches' hands.

Coach White said, "Nice game tonight, Cade. That was a great finish."

"Thanks. It was scary for a while, but we really came together down the stretch."

Coach Jenkins nodded and said, "You sure did." He then said, "Coach White and I don't want to take too much of your time, but we would each like to talk with you for a few minutes if that's okay with you, Cade."

"Sure," said Cade.

"All right, well, why don't you two talk for a few minutes and then you and I can talk?"

Cade said, "All right," and he and Coach White sat down in two seats in front of them.

Del and Rich Jenkins stepped away from Cade and Coach White. They spoke for a couple of minutes. A few minutes later Jim walked Cade over to Del and Coach Jenkins and said, "All yours, Coach." Coach White shook hands with Cade and said, "Good luck at State next week. We'll be in touch."

Del and Jim White sat down as Cade and Rich Jenkins stepped away to find a seat.

Del asked, "Are you guys going to make an offer to Cade?"

Jim responded, "Yeah, I think so."

Del said, "It would mean the world to him. He's a good kid. He's just had it in his head for so long that he has to be 'The Man,' that sometimes he forgets the team aspects. But you saw at the end tonight what he's capable of when he plays the right way. And quite honestly, you didn't see his best strength—his ability to score. That kid can fill it up."

"I know," said Jim. "I've seen the film. You're right. He certainly can fill it up. I'll admit though, we were a little worried about just what you're talking about. We want kids who will buy into team. They need individual skills, absolutely. But if they aren't going to play within the framework and concept of team, we don't want them."

"I have tried to tell Cade that for two years. I saw spurts of it, but it just hasn't been there consistently. Tonight, though, I saw something in him I had never seen before."

"What's that?" asked Jim.

"He loved the feeling he had playing as a great teammate. You should have seen him in the locker room after the game. He was all-in with his teammates. He got pretty emotional with his teammates about how he has been through the years. He apologized to them and to Remington. But this time, he meant it. Then after everyone came out here to see their families, he told me he loved this team feeling, and he wanted a lot more of it. He then apologized to me for not understanding before. He got pretty emotional again. I think he really turned a corner."

Coach White said, "That's huge when that happens. When someone with all that physical skill who has played selfishly their whole life turns the corner and figures out that the team game is so much more fun and fulfilling, that the 'we' is bigger than 'me,' that's when they start to really become something. It'll be interesting to see how he plays next week."

Del said, "I know. I'm just hoping it wasn't just words like in the past. I don't think it will be, though, based on what I saw, heard, and just felt from him in there. I think he got it today."

Coach Jenkins and Cade walked back over to Del and Jim White, who stood up as they approached. Cade shook hands with both coaches again. Jim White said, "All right, well, I know you've got a couple other guys over there who want to talk to you," motioning to Pat Baker talking to Remington. "The two of us may not be able to compete with the size of their school and the fact that they're D1, but we can offer you something they can't."

Cade nodded as if he understood, but inside, he was wondering what the coach was talking about. Coach White continued, "You won't get lost in the shuffle with us. You won't just be a piece of meat. Quite honestly, Cade, you'll struggle to get minutes there, at least early on. I think Coach Jenkins will agree with me that at each of our schools, you'll have a chance to play and play right away. If U of M is truly interested in you, you'll have to ask yourself if playing is more important than just being part of a program. I'm not saying you won't be able to work yourself into it in the next few years at the U. You might be able to. But at our two schools, you'll have a shot the moment you arrive. It's certainly something to think about."

Cade nodded and said, "All right. That's good to know. Thanks."

They all shook hands, and the coaches wished Cade good luck again and told him they'd be in touch. Del and Cade turned and headed towards Pat Baker and Travis Lake. Del said, "Well, what did you think?"

Cade said, "It was cool. I liked both of them. They were really nice. I could see playing for either of them."

"Good," said Del. "They are both good guys and good coaches, and academically, their schools are two of the best schools in Montana. Heck, they're two of the best schools in the nation. You can't go wrong with either of them."

"Yeah, that's what I've heard," said Cade.

"Okay," said Del. "Now you get to talk to U of M. Coach Baker is another good guy and good coach. This is a huge step up from Rocky and Tech in terms of athletics. Those two schools are every bit as good, if not better, academically as U of M. But athletically, it's a whole different ball game at U of M."

The two of them walked over to Coach Baker and Coach Lake. Coach Baker was still talking with Remington, so Coach Lake stepped over, shook Cade's hand and said. "Cade, I'm Coach Travis Lake with the University of Montana."

Cade shook his hand and said, "Nice to meet you, Coach."

Coach Lake said, "Congratulations on getting to the state tournament!"

Cade said, "Thanks. That's been our goal all year long from day one. Coach wrote 'Get to State' on the whiteboard before our first practice. And that's been pretty much our main focus every night. In some ways, I can't believe it just happened."

"Nothing like seeing one of your goals come true after all the hard work it took to get there," said Coach Lake.

As he said this, the head coach, Pat Baker, stepped up to them along with Remington. As he got up to Cade, Coach Baker extended his hand out to shake Cade's hand. He said, "Hi, Cade. I'm Coach Baker from the University of Montana."

Cade said, "Nice to meet you, Coach."

Coach Baker shook Del's hand as well, saying, "Nice game tonight, Coach."

Del said, "Thanks, Coach."

Coach Baker looked at Cade and Remington and said, "With a couple of guys like this on your team, you can make some noise next week, huh?"

Del said, "We're sure hoping to."

Coach Baker turned back to Remington and said, "All right, well, we will get in touch with you right after the state tournament. We want to start the process with you and see about getting you over to our camp this summer. How does that sound?"

"Great!" said Remington. "I'd like that a lot."

"All right then. Well, good luck next week. One of us will be there to watch you. We're looking forward to seeing you play a lot more."

"Okay. Thanks, Coach," said Remington.

Del said, "You need to hustle up and get showered, Rem."

Remington said, "Okay, Coach." He turned away from them, fist-bumped Cade, smiled, and whispered, "Knock 'em dead, Cade." He and Del headed for the locker room.

Cade smiled and turned to Coach Baker. Coach Baker motioned for him to sit down. He said, "That was quite an impressive game, Cade."

Cade said, "Thanks."

Coach Baker continued, "You know what I was most impressed with?"

Cade shook his head no.

"I was impressed with how late in the game, as frustrated as you had been earlier, you didn't try to force everything, like you had been earlier. You adjusted to what Gallatin was doing to you. You realized your team needed you to get all of them involved and play to their strengths, rather than try to force your strengths and your will on them. That's the mark of a smart player who has figured out that this is a team game. 'We win together, and we lose together. It's not about me. It's about us.' I loved seeing you think that way."

Cade smiled and in the tiniest of split seconds thought to himself, "If only that were true. If only that were how I usually thought. I just finally got it cuz Coach wouldn't let me play if I didn't. I can't believe a college coach is saying this stuff. I only thought Coach Brooks said that stuff to get me to play with my teammates. I didn't think college coaches cared about that stuff."

What Cade said, though, was "Well, I knew that the way they were defending me, I couldn't get shots, but my teammates had great looks. We've got a good team, and I trust them to hit their shots."

"Trust," said Coach Baker. "That's the key. If teammates don't trust one another, they're not going to be successful. You have to be able to trust them, and they have to be able to trust you. And if coaches can't trust players to do the right thing, the players can't be on the floor."

It was like Coach Brooks was sitting there talking to Cade. Cade had heard Coach Brooks say that kind of stuff so many times in the last few years. He didn't really think much of it when Coach Brooks said it, though. He just figured he was trying to make Cade play his way. He thought, "Maybe Coach Brooks knows more than I ever thought he knew."

Coach Baker continued, "Cade, I'm going to be honest with you. We have one scholarship spot left open. I always like to leave one open late for a kid who just flew under our radar over the last couple of years. I had another kid in mind from over near Seattle that I have been considering offering it to. He's a great team player, and the kind of kid who any coach would want to coach and any player would want to play with. But quite honestly, I usually like to have a homegrown Montana boy fill that spot, and after watching you today, I'm thinking of you instead. I saw something in you that I didn't see in the film that Coach Brooks sent us."

Cade had heard Del tell him earlier about sending them film. He hadn't realized Coach had done that. He thought, "I didn't know he would do that for me."

Coach Baker continued, "On film I saw a player with a lot of skill, a player who could score really well. But I didn't see a player all that committed to his teammates. I didn't see a player focused on what was best for the team. I rarely saw you interact with your teammates. I also know that film doesn't always show that kind of stuff, so I thought I should see for myself. Quite honestly, my thoughts were being confirmed in the first three quarters of the game. But in that fourth quarter, that's when I saw what you're really capable of."

Coach Baker paused and intently looked Cade in the eyes. "Cade, you had the biggest impact on your team without ever scoring a point. I knew you could shoot, attack, and finish. What I didn't know is if you could play as a great team player, a great teammate. But you sure showed me that in the last four minutes of the game. The moment you gave up 'you' for 'team,' everything clicked for you, your team, and actually, for me, too. That's when I thought, 'I need to think about getting this kid on campus.'"

Coach Baker let his words sink in. He then said, "Cade, I'm not going to make you any promises, and I know you've got a state tournament to think about. But after your season, I want to get you on campus for a visit and put you through a workout with us. If you'd be interested in that last spot on our roster, I'd be interested in having you fill it. Again, this is not a guarantee or an offer. But I want to know if you would be interested. Understand that the last spot on a roster means you probably won't see much game action, at least not right away. We'd probably red-shirt you for your freshman year. You understand what that means?"

Chapter 25

Cade said, "Yeah, that I'd practice and work out with you guys, but I wouldn't play or travel with the team."

"Exactly. You would be working on developing your game and getting used to the college experience. Then, your sophomore year becomes like your freshman year in that you'll still have four years of eligibility left. I can't guarantee that you'll play in that time, either. You may develop; you may not. Other players may develop and they may not, and we'll be recruiting other guys each year, all looking to play. But you will have your shot and a chance. And that's what I would be offering you. I don't want you to give me an answer now. I want you to think about it. Let's get you and your parents on campus and talk with them, too. It's a big step and a big decision."

Cade nodded as Coach Baker continued. "I saw you talking to the guys from Rocky and Tech." Cade was worried that might have made Coach Baker upset. Coach continued, "Those are great schools, and they might be perfect for you. I could see you playing at either of those schools, having a great career, and getting a great education. You would have a much better chance of playing at those two schools than with us. And you'd have that chance a lot earlier with them. You might not have to red-shirt with them either. I would not begrudge you one bit deciding to go to one of those two schools. Kids play basketball to *play*, not to sit and watch, so I would totally get it. But if you would like to be part of the best program in the state, a D1 program that travels all around the country, plays against some of the best teams and best talent in the country, then you really need to think about what I'm saying. Let's talk after the state tournament, set up a campus visit, and see where your mind is at, okay?"

Cade said, "Absolutely, Coach. I'd love to do that!"

"All right, Cade," said Coach Baker. "I'm excited for you. Best of luck next week at the state tournament. I'm not sure if I will be there next week, but Coach Lake or one of my other assistants will be there if I can't make it. We'll be in touch, all right?"

Cade said, "All right. Thanks, Coach." Coach Baker smiled, shook Cade's hand, and turned and headed to find his seat to watch the next game.

Cade turned and headed towards the locker room. He was so excited he didn't know what to think or do. "Holy cow," he thought. "An hour ago, I was nothing. Nobody knew me or cared about me. And now, I have three schools, one of them being U of M, that are interested in me playing for them. And all they could talk about was the last four minutes of that game. The four minutes when I didn't score. How crazy is that? All they talked about was being a great teammate. Why haven't I played that way sooner?

He stopped before stepping through the locker room door. "Gosh, if I would have played that way sooner, maybe I would have had more schools looking at me. Coach Baker was already talking to Remington, and he's just a junior. But he plays that way all the time. Maybe that's what these colleges want."

He stepped through the locker room door, and Coach Brooks was packing up his briefcase. Remington had showered, dressed, and was in front of a mirror combing his hair. Cade smiled and said, "Forget about it, Rem. You're not that pretty."

Remington said, "That's why I gotta' get in front of the mirror and take care of business. But now," and he turned around to face Cade, "I'm smokin'! Look out ladies. Here comes Remington Roberts," he said with a laugh.

Cade laughed and said, "Yeah, look out is right, as in 'Look out because the ugliest dude in the world is here.'" They both laughed.

Remington said, "So what did Coach Baker say?"

Cade started telling Remington all about their conversation and the conversations with the other two coaches as they headed out the door and towards where the team was sitting. Del followed them, just catching bits and pieces of their conversation. He thought, "They sound like two best friends sharing some of the most exciting news they've ever had. Why couldn't Cade have been this way all along? Why did he have to fight being a teammate, a friend to these guys all these years? If he'd have opened his eyes, his mind, his heart to this last year, who knows where it would have taken him and us?"

He heard them comparing what Coach Baker had told each of them. Del could see and hear the excitement that each of them felt for the opportunities that were being presented to them. Del thought. "Maybe he gets it now."

Del paused in his thoughts, wishing that Cade had come around to this way of thinking and playing sooner. Del thought, "Oh well, if he really has turned a corner, then it's like they always say—better late than never."

Ideas to Consider:

- **What were the college coaches most impressed with about how Cade played? What does Cade wish he had done differently through the years?**
- **What lesson can you take away from Cade's situation and the college coaches' comments to him? Do you think college coaches really do think this way?**

Chapter 26

As Cade and Remington made their way out and into the stands, various friends and family were there to greet them with smiles, hugs, and statements of "Congratulations!" They both soaked it all in. Cade found his parents and hugged them both and sat down to watch the next game with them.

Remington's parents met him after he made his way through a throng of friends all high-fiving him and talking about how well he played and how exciting it was for them to be going to the state tournament the following weekend. Remington smiled a lot, tried to talk about it, but also was a bit embarrassed at all the attention he was receiving.

As strange as it felt for him as a 17-year-old kid, he just wanted to get through the crowd to his dad and his mom. He especially wanted to talk to his dad. Steve Roberts had been Remington's coach his entire young life until high school. He had been a successful high-school coach himself in both Montana and Arizona, so he was able to help give a lot of basketball knowledge and general athletic ideas to Remington from a young age. While they had a great relationship in every way, basketball was their first and probably their tightest bond. Remington wanted to share this incredible moment with him.

When he got to his parents, Remington hugged his mom, Marie, first. She said, "Congratulations, Rem. You were awesome!"

He said, "Thanks, Mom. That was so cool."

As he broke away from her and reached for his dad, he could see tears in his dad's eyes. Steve reached his arms around Remington and gave him a great bear-hug. Steve said into his ear, "Congrats, Son. You know I am always proud of you, but I am even more proud of you today. Look what you accomplished. You took your game, and you took your team to a whole new level. I couldn't be happier for you. I love you, Buddy."

Chapter 26

Remington now had tears in his eyes, too, and he said, "Thanks, Dad. I love you, too." As Steve started to pull away from him, Remington held him for a second longer and said into his dad's ear, "And thanks for always being there for me, always pushing me to be my best, always helping me through everything. Thanks for showing me this game. I love playing basketball so much. I couldn't have done any of this without you. I don't know if I would have ever fallen in love with basketball if it wasn't for you."

Steve said, "Oh, I'm sure you would have. It's in your blood. I was just there to give you a little nudge in that direction." They both smiled and pulled away from each other.

Marie said, "We saw you talking to the U of M coach. How did that go?"

"Great!" said Remington. "They want me to come to their camp this summer and do a campus visit."

Steve said, "That's awesome! U of M is such a great school, and their team is solid. You would love it there."

"Yeah, I know," said Remington. "Ever since you took me to those football games there when I was little, I've thought it would be cool to go there."

Steve could sense something in Remington's voice, and said, "But... ?"

Remington looked up at his dad and said, "But I just wonder if there might be other schools out there that would be interested in me."

"Oh, I imagine there will be," said Steve. "Who are you wondering about?" Steve figured he knew what schools Remington would say, but he wanted to hear it from Remington.

"I don't know. Gonzaga, maybe. ASU, UW or Oregon." He paused for a moment and then said, "Duke?" Ever since he was little, playing at Duke for Coach K had been his dream. Again, Steve was the catalyst for that. Steve had been a huge Duke fan ever since the 1980s when Coach K had started making Duke the program it had become. Remington's favorite team became Duke, too.

Steve said, "Well, with the year you've had, the tournament you just had, and whatever happens next week, you will certainly be on people's radars. Not sure if those schools will be on that list, but maybe they will be. The key will be whatever you do this summer on your AAU team. Those tournaments you're going to play at in Seattle, Vegas, and LA will be key. Not sure

153

if Duke will be at those, and I don't know if you have Duke-level of abilities. But the other four should be at those tournaments, and I think you're showing you could play at those schools. You still have a lot of work to do to get to their levels, and as a Montana kid you need to prove even more to them. But that's never stopped you before, and you never shied away from that kind of challenge, so I like your odds."

Marie said, "When is the camp at U of M?"

Remington said, "Oh, I don't know. He didn't say. He said they'll get in touch with me after the state tournament to start setting it up."

She said, "Okay. Well, this is all so exciting." She paused and then asked, "Are you hungry?"

"Starving," said Remington. "Can I have a little money to go get something to eat?"

Marie said, "How did I know?" She reached into her pocket and pulled out a twenty-dollar bill, handed it to him and said, "Here you go. I want change back, though."

Just as Marie handed him the money, Jenny Jones walked up and said, "Oh, hi Mrs. Roberts. Great timing! Are you handing out money to everyone?!"

They all laughed, and Marie said, "Hi Jenny. No, I'm just handing it out to beggars like Remington."

Jenny laughed, turned to Remington, reached out to give him a big hug, and yelled, *"AHHHHH!* You did it! Congratulations! I knew you would. You were awesome!"

Remington said, "Thanks, Jen." It felt so good to hold her, but it was also very awkward. He didn't know how she felt about him, so he didn't know how long he should hug her. Besides, his parents were standing right there and he wondered if they would be able to tell what he was thinking and feeling and—"*ARRGGHHH!* What the hell am I doing?" he thought. "Why am I thinking this way? Get it together." He let go of Jenny.

He said, "It was so much fun. I'm so glad you were here to see it."

She said, "Are you kidding? I wouldn't have missed this for anything. We had so much fun in the student section. Everyone kept talking about how great you were, and I kept saying, 'Yep. That's my best friend. Taught him everything he knows.'" She laughed.

Remington laughed, too, but he thought, "Best friend. Yeah, that's what we are—best friends. I guess that's the only way she thinks of me."

Remington quickly snapped out of that thought and said, "Yeah, it looked like you guys were having a blast up there. There were moments when I was wishing I was up there with you guys instead of down on the court."

Jenny looked around, leaned in a little closer to all of them, and said, "You mean the moments where Cade was playing like a totally selfish jerk?" She looked disgusted. "Oh wait, that was the whole game, so I guess it couldn't have been then."

Remington immediately came back with, "Hey, wait a minute. Did you see the last four minutes of the game? He was awesome. In fact, if he didn't play that way for those last four minutes, we wouldn't have won that game."

Before Jenny could respond, Steve said, "You're absolutely right, Rem. He was awesome those last four minutes. But you're also absolutely right when you say, 'if he didn't play that way.' Once he figured that out, he was a totally different player, and you guys became a totally different team. I'm just glad he figured it out before it was too late."

"Me too," said Remington. "He was so much fun to play with those last four minutes. That's the guy I've always wanted to play with through these years. You should have heard him in the locker room afterward, too. He was like a totally different person. It was awesome."

"Oh, really," said Jenny. "Do tell."

"Sorry, Jen, but I can't," said Remington. "The locker room is sacred. You know how people say, 'What happens in Vegas, stays in Vegas'? Well, 'What happens in the locker room, stays in the locker room.'"

She said, "That's a nice thought, Rem, but I know way too many guys who have not lived by that concept. We hear way too often about what happened in a locker room, and usually, it's things I never wanted to hear about." They all laughed.

Remington said, "All right, well, I'm starving, so I wanna' get a bite to eat. Jen, you want to come with?"

"Sure," she said.

Remington turned to his folks and said, "All right, we'll see you later."

Marie said, "All right, honey. Your dad and I are going to head home. Have fun. Keep in touch about when you will be home, okay?"

"Okay, Mom."

Marie said, "Nice to see you again, Jenny. Keep an eye on this boy, will you?"

Jenny wanted to say, "I'll keep both eyes on him. I love looking at him," but of course she couldn't do that. Instead she just smiled and said, "Well, I guess I'll have to if you're asking."

Steve reached out and gave Remington a hug and whispered into his ear, "See you later, Buddy. Love you."

Remington whispered back, "Love you, too, Dad."

This time it was Steve who held on a second longer, and he whispered in Remington's ear, "She's a keeper, Son."

Remington pulled away from his dad, looked at him with a confused look, and said, "What?"

Steve smiled at him and said, "See ya'. See ya' later, Jenny." He turned with Marie and headed towards the exit.

Remington stood for a second and wondered what the heck his dad meant. Had he seen how Remington reacted when Jenny hugged him? "Does dad know something that I don't know? Did Jenny say something to them? What the heck is going on?"

Jenny grabbed his hand and jarred him out of his thoughts. "Come on," she said. "Let's go get something to eat."

Ideas to Consider:

- What is Remington's biggest dream for his future? What does his dad think of his dream? What does his dad say Remington needs to do to try to achieve it?
- What dreams do you have for your future? What do you need to do to achieve them? What steps can you start taking today to begin your quest to achieve them?

Chapter 27

As Remington and Jenny walked to the concession stand, Remington couldn't get his dad's words out of his head—"She's a keeper, Son."

"What the heck was he talking about?" thought Remington. "Does he know how I feel about her? Is it obvious? Who else knows?" Remington looked at Jenny as they walked. Then another thought came to him. "Can she tell how I feel? Oh no, is it obvious to her, too?"

As he looked at her, she looked at him and smiled, saying, "I can't believe you're going to state next week. That is so awesome! I wonder if they'll cancel school on Thursday. We already have Friday off for a teacher work day. I hope they give us Thursday off, too."

Remington replied, "Yeah, I hope so, too. But I don't know. They've never done anything like that before." He paused and then added, "Then again, I can't remember the last time a team in any of our sports has made it to the state tournament."

Jenny said, "Well, even if they don't give us the day off, I'm going. I have plenty of absences to go before I get dinged, so I'm going."

"Will your parents let you?" asked Remington.

"Are you kidding?" she said. "They'll be the ones who will take me! They love basketball. You know my dad used to play and how much he loves watching you play. We talk about you all the time. Remington Roberts is one of the most popular topics around our dinner table."

Remington was a bit taken aback by this. It made him feel good to know that Jenny's parents liked him so much. They were really nice people, and he always liked talking hoops with her dad. He just didn't realize they talked about him when he wasn't there. He said, "What is wrong with you guys? You don't have anything better to talk about than me?"

Chapter 27

They were now at the back of the line at the concession stand. Jenny said, "What could be better than talking about you?" Remington was looking at her when she said it, and he couldn't help but noticing a different look on her face as she said it. He didn't know how to read that look. He had never seen it from her before. And then, almost as if she could read his thoughts, her face showed she was a little embarrassed by what she said. Seemingly flustered, she added, "I mean, you're the best basketball player our school has seen in a long time. Everyone wants to talk about you." She smiled and looked like her usual self.

Remington thought, "What just happened? What was she saying? Did she have feelings more than just being my friend? Is she thinking about me the way I'm thinking about her?"

Of course, he couldn't speak any of those thoughts out loud. He wanted to ask her, but he didn't dare. "What if she doesn't feel that way about me? What if it's just me? She's been my best friend for years. I don't want to ruin that. Then again, I don't want to just be her best friend. I want more. *Arrgghh!* What should I do?"

Jenny was waiting for a response, but she sensed he was lost in his thoughts. "What is he thinking?" she wondered. "Can he tell how I'm feeling about him? Oh, no. I screwed up. He can tell I like him. He can tell I want to be more than friends. What have I done? I don't want to screw up our friendship, but I want to be more than friends. Do I dare tell him? No, I can't do that. I would hate for him to know and then not like me anymore. *Arrgghh!* What should I do?"

They were behind four people in line at the concession stand. Remington looked up at the board above the cashier's head and said to Jenny, "What do you want?"

She paused for a minute wondering what he was asking her. She realized he was only asking about what she wanted to order to eat. She said, "I'm not sure. What are you getting?" She then thought, "Phew, he didn't catch it. Maybe he doesn't know how I feel after all."

Remington replied, "I'm not sure. I've been thinking about pizza all day, but they don't have any here. Maybe I'll get a burger."

Jenny said, "Oh yeah, pizza sounds really good. I wish they had pizza, too." She paused and said, "I tell you what. You get a burger, I'll get fries, and we can split them both. Then, tonight, when we get back to Discovery, we can go to Pizza Hut. My treat for the best basketball player in Montana."

Remington smiled and said, "Oh, is Josh McKinney going to join us?"

Jenny said, "Who's Josh McKinney?"

Remington said, "The best basketball player in Montana. He plays at Big Sky over in Missoula."

She hit Remington in the arm and said, "No, dummy. You're the best basketball player in Montana. At least you're the best to me." As the words escaped her mouth, she could feel that they sounded like more than just a statement about how great a basketball player Remington was. She felt she needed to pull the words back. Of course, they were already out there, so the only thing she could do was add, "Well, and in everyone else's mind here at this tournament." She smiled at him, hoping he didn't catch her feelings for him again. "Keep it together, Jenny," she said to herself.

Remington said, "Well, then you and everyone else at this tournament haven't seen Josh McKinney play. That kid is unreal. He's got a full ride to Gonzaga next year."

"Well, then maybe you'll be his teammate the following year," she said. "Gonzaga's one of your schools you'd like to go to, right?"

"Absolutely," said Remington. "It's at the top of my list." He caught himself and said, "Well, Duke's at the top of the list, but that's not going to happen."

"Why not?"

"Are you kidding?" he asked. "It's Duke. It's Coach K. It's the best program in the nation year in and year out. Maybe you haven't noticed, but they aren't beating down the doors to come out to my games or to get video on me."

Jenny looked him in the eyes and said, "Is that where you really want to go?"

Remington said, "Yeah, absolutely. It's been my #1 goal since I was in 4th grade. My dad always loved Duke because of Coach K, so ever since I can remember, they've been my favorite team, too." He paused and said, "Did you know that the night I was born, I sat on my dad's lap—well, more like slept on his chest—watching a Duke game?"

"Uh, yeah, I knew that," said Jenny. "You've only told me that like a thousand times."

"Well, of course, I don't remember it because, well, you know, I had just been born a few hours earlier. But Duke has been ingrained in me my entire life as the ultimate place to go to school and play basketball. You know, it's funny. Most guys dream of playing in the NBA. I dream of playing at Duke." He paused and then said, "Don't get me wrong. I'd love to play in the NBA. But the dream has always been Duke."

"Well then you need to go to Duke," said Jenny.

Remington just said, "Ha!" It wasn't so much Jenny's words that hit him. It was her matter-of-fact tone. It was the way she said it, as if since he wanted to go play basketball at Duke, he should just go play basketball at Duke. He said, "Yeah right. I just need to go to Duke." But the tone of his voice said there was no way he was going to be going to Duke.

They were now the next people in line to order. She put her hand on his arm in the gentlest, yet assured way, and said, "Rem, if you want to go to Duke that badly, you need to go Duke. You need to do everything in your power to get there. It's your dream. Why would you give up on your dream this far away from it? Because you live in Montana? So what! You just said that Josh guy is going to Gonzaga. Gonzaga is one of the best teams in the nation."

"Yeah," he said. "They've been in the top 20 every year for like 20 years now. They even played Duke in the National Championship game a few years ago."

Jenny said, "Right. They are on that same kind of level as Duke, or at least really close. And a Montana kid is going there. If that kid can go to Gonzaga, why can't you go to Duke?"

Remington looked at her, but he didn't have a response. In fact, what she said made perfect sense. And yet, it didn't. Or did it? On the one hand, Duke is a great school and a great basketball program, one of the best in the country. Yet, Gonzaga was those exact same things. If a Montana kid could go to Gonzaga, why couldn't he go to Duke? On the other hand, Duke was all the way on the other side of the country. They played in the ACC, the best basketball conference in the NCAA. There's no way a Montana kid was going to go there. Then he thought, "Wait a minute. Darius Jones just went to Florida State and he's from Montana. They're in the ACC, and they've been just about as good as Duke the last few years. Heck, at times they've been better than Duke. If Darius could go to Florida State, why couldn't I go to Duke?"

Jenny could see the wheels turning in Remington's head. She leaned her head to get into his sight line while he was lost in his thoughts. "Rem? Hello. Earth to Remington."

Remington snapped out of it looked at her and said, "Sorry, but you got me thinking. Maybe I can go to Duke. Maybe I could make it there. I would have to work awfully hard, but who knows? Maybe I could get there."

Now it was Jenny's turn to say, "Absolutely." She smiled after she said it and then said, "If that's what you want, go for it. If you make it, it would be so awesome."

Remington then had a different look in his eyes as he said, "But what if I don't make it?"

She said, "Then you don't make it. But at least you tried. At least you gave it everything you had. At least you gave yourself a legitimate shot at your dream." She paused and then said, "My mom always says, 'Jenny, you can do anything you set your mind to. Shoot for the moon.' And when I would come back with, 'What if I don't make it?' She would say, 'Then you'll land in the stars. Not a bad place to end up, huh?' Well, Rem, shoot for the moon. Try going to Duke. If you don't make it, you'll end up at another great place… like Gonzaga." She paused, then added, "But at least you'll know you tried. After all, isn't that what it's all about?"

They were now at the front of the line, and Remington ordered a burger and fries. Jenny got out some money, and he said, "I got this. It's on me."

She smiled at him and then said, "You mean it's on your mom, right?"

They both laughed as he realized he'd been caught. "Oh yeah, right. Well, since that's the case, do you want anything else?!"

They laughed again, and she said, "Wanna' split a milkshake?"

"Sure," he said. "Chocolate?"

"Yeah, that'd be great," Jenny replied.

He ordered the milkshake, too. When their food came, they headed back into the seats to watch the game that was being played. They went up to the balcony to get away from people and to have a little space to spread out and eat. They ate and talked about many things, mainly basketball-related. Remington thought how lucky he was to have Jenny as a friend. She loved talking basketball with him. At least she acted like she did. Truth be told, she did more listening than talking about basketball, but that was one of the things he loved about her.

Remington paused as that thought hit him again. "One of things I love about her. Do I mean that? Do I love her? Of course, I have always loved her the way any friend loves a friend. But do I actually love her in the other way?"

He was so torn about his feelings for Jenny. He just didn't know what he was feeling. He then thought, "Get it together, Rem. You've got a state tournament to play in next week. Stay focused on what's most important." As he finished that thought, he looked at Jenny eating her French fries and watching the game and thought, "But I sure do like thinking about her."

Ideas to Consider:

- What does Jenny tell Remington about his dream to go to Duke? How does he react?
- Is it a good thing to have big dreams, or should you keep your dreams smaller, so you aren't crushed if they don't come true? What are the pros and cons of each way of thinking and dreaming?

Chapter 28

Goals are a tricky thing. So often, as one is achieved, a new one pops up to take its place. After the Wolves achieved their goal of getting to the state tournament, they had a new goal of placing at state or even, dare they dream it, winning the state championship. However, no matter what they would accomplish at the state tournament, no one could ever take this moment away from them. They had set out on a journey with one goal in mind—Getting to the State Tournament—TOGETHER. They had achieved that. Everything else was gravy.

The state tournament did not go the way they had hoped. Of course, every team at the tournament dreams of winning a state championship, and every team there is good enough to win it. But in most state tournaments around the country, there are usually a couple of teams that stand a bit above the rest in terms of their chances of winning it. This year the Montana Class A State Tournament was no exception. The two best teams in the state, Longbow and Grinnell Point, met in the championship game as most people had predicted. Longbow edged out Grinnell Point in a hard-fought contest, winning their first state championship in a decade.

Sacajawea had their struggles at state. They battled hard in their Thursday afternoon contest against Mineral County from the far west side of the state. But they could never overcome a poor first half performance, and they ended up losing by 9. In their second game against Bighorn the following morning, they had the opposite problem. They came out strong and held an 8-point lead at the half. However, they were fatigued from the game the day before, and they ran out of gas, losing by 7.

They were disappointed in themselves for not placing in the top 3 and for not even getting to the Saturday games. But at the same time, they felt a satisfaction in achieving their original goal—getting to state—and the fulfillment of that goal in the best way possible—TOGETHER! While they wanted more in terms of state placing, they actually got so much more than

Chapter 28

they ever bargained for. They grew together, struggled along the way, fought, argued, learned to love one another like brothers and friends, and ultimately, became the greatest thing they could become—a TEAM. It couldn't get much better than that.

Del had worked to create a team out of a group of players with their own individual skills and personalities. While he succeeded for the most part, he knew he didn't do all that he should have with Cade through the years. It was a costly mistake, but one that he would learn from and try to not let happen again. With most of this year's players coming back next year, Del was excited about the prospects of getting back to the tournament, and with Remington blossoming into one of the best players in the state, anything was possible next year.

For Cade, after all of his me-first attitude displays through the years, he finally figured it out. He had a state tournament that showed what he could truly be. He scored 21 and 18 points in their two games at the tournament. More importantly, he had 4 assists in the first game and 6 assists in his final high school game, the most assists he ever had in a game. This was the best basketball Cade had ever played, and he did it within the concept of what was best for the team. He engaged with every one of his teammates, high-fiving, laughing, joking, and just having a great time with them. He was the Cade they had all hoped he would be when they started their journey at the beginning of the year. While they wished he would have been this way all year, they were glad to have him this way at the end of it.

Cade, too, loved the way he had become. Even though they lost their two games, he found that the joy in playing the game truly lies in playing the game with your teammates. He found that the more he gave to them, the more he got back from them, and the more he liked it. He, too, wished he would have found this out sooner, but he also didn't dwell on it. He realized that, if he was going to play in college, this is who he needed to be. But now, he actually wanted to be that guy. He had much more fun playing that way. He just hoped that a college would take a chance on him, so he could put into play what he had finally learned.

Two months later, Cade got his wish. Well, at least he got part of his wish. The only D1 school to show interest in him remained the University of Montana, and they offered him the last scholarship spot on the team. Coach Baker told Cade that he would red-shirt for his freshmen year and see how things progressed. If he continued to develop, he might work his way into a spot on the team and become a key cog in the wheel, but nothing was guaranteed.

Other smaller schools recruited Cade after the state tournament, too. However, the two schools that first spoke to him at the Divisional Tournament, Rocky Mountain and Montana Tech, pursued him the most, and Cade appreciated their interest in him more than the rest. They had seen things they liked at the Divisional Tournament, but at the State Tournament, they saw what they really wanted to see—a kid who could be committed to his teammates and who could blend his own strong individual skills with what the team needed from him.

Rocky and Tech offered him the maximum athletic scholarship money they could offer someone to play basketball at their school. Because of his outstanding grades, they were also able to offer him the maximum academic scholarship money, too. Cade was in a nice position, with two schools wanting him badly. He also had a newfound love for playing a team game. He felt if he played at U of M, he wouldn't get to experience that feeling right away. In fact, he might never get to experience it.

At Tech or Rocky, Cade knew he would get to be a part of the team right from the start. He just wanted so much more of that feeling, and he felt that one of those two schools would offer a much better chance for him to experience it. It was a tough decision, but in the end, he chose Montana Tech. He was interested in the sciences and possibly engineering, and Tech was one of the best schools in the nation in those areas. It felt like a better fit for Cade. He was excited about his future.

As for the rest of the members of the team, they had solid performances at the state tournament. Billy Thompson finished out his basketball career with games of 8 and 10 points. He was headed to Minot State University in North Dakota the next year to play football. He would be able to take all that he learned in basketball and apply it to football and academics.

All of the younger players found the state experience to be one of the best things they had ever been a part of, and they couldn't wait to get back there the next year. They continued to grow their love for the game, the competition, and each other during the week of the state tournament. While they would have loved to have placed in the top three and receive a trophy, they knew they had nothing to be ashamed of. They just ran into two of the best teams in the state and couldn't quite get over the hump and win.

Chapter 28

But they got a taste of what it takes to get to the state tournament and what it would take for them to have success once they got there. They all left the tournament with a mission in mind to do all that they could to begin working on getting back to state and getting hardware to bring home. They headed home with a newfound purpose and plan to become the best they could be over the next year and get back to state and finish things off as State Champions.

As for Remington, he had another outstanding tournament, garnering the attention of every college coach and scout in attendance with his 16-point, 11-assist, 6-rebound, and 4-steals game in the opener. He then completely blew them away with his 14 assists in the final game, to go along with 15 points. The contacts from those schools and others increased in the weeks after the tournament. Remington was now on the radar of every school in the western part of the country, as well as some on the east coast.

He even had a letter from Duke signed by Coach K! Remington understood that they probably send out hundreds of those letters to kids all around the country. Whether he was truly on Coach K's radar or not didn't really matter. He had his autograph, and for now that was as good as it got. When he opened the letter and read it, he showed it to his parents. They were almost as excited as he was. He then said, "I have to show this to Jenny."

He texted her to see if she was home, and she was. She lived just a couple of blocks away, and he headed out the door, running all the way to her house. When she opened the door, she said, "What is going on? Why are you out of breath? What happened?"

He handed her the letter and said, "Look what came in the mail today!"

As she saw the letterhead, she smiled. She read the letter and saw Coach K's signature, looked up at Remington, smiled and said, "That is so cool! You see; I told you. You can do this Rem!" She reached her arms out around him and gave him a big hug.

He hugged her back and said, "I can't believe it. I mean, I know it's just a form letter, but still, it's Duke. It's Coach K, and I think he really signed it."

Jenny looked at the letter again and said, "I think you're right about the signature, but I think you're wrong about the form letter."

He looked confused and said, "Why? What makes you say that?"

"Well, look what he says about your tournament. He knew you had all those assists. He said he values team-first players, and that you obviously fit that mold." Jenny looked at him and said, "Rem, I don't think this is a form letter. I think Coach K or someone there found out about you, checked out your tournament, and decided they needed to take a closer look."

Remington said, "Really? You really think so?"

"Yeah, I do," she said. "It might not have been Coach K. It might have been another coach or someone on their staff. I imagine at a place like that, they have a lot of people who work for them who do those kinds of things. But someone did it, put it into a letter, handed it to Coach K to sign, and then mailed it to you."

She paused as she saw Remington thinking. Then she said, "Rem, you're knocking on their door. As good as you are, as good a teammate as you are, and as good a student as you are, you have all that it takes to walk through that door. You have to focus everything you've got—basketball, weight room, and studying—this spring and summer to make sure that they have no choice but to turn around and start knocking on your door, too."

He looked up at her, smiled as big a smile as he could, and reached out and gave her another big hug. He said, "Come on, let's go to Dairy Queen. It's on me."

"I never turn down Dairy Queen!" said Jenny.

They walked the two blocks to the Dairy Queen, talking the entire time about Duke, Coach K, and some of the great players that had played there. Remington realized that the entire time, Jenny had never tried to change the conversation to something else. She was interested, or at least pretended to be interested, in everything he was saying. Again, Remington realized that these were the kinds of things that he loved about her.

As they sat eating their ice cream cones, and Remington realized how he was feeling about Jenny, he had an uncharacteristic moment come to him, take him over, and propel him to a place he'd never been before. "What are you doing tonight?" he asked her.

"Nothing," she said. "No plans yet. April and I were thinking of just hanging out and watching TV, but she might have to stay home and babysit, so I don't know if we will. Why?"

Chapter 28

He couldn't believe he was doing it, but Remington said, "Do you want to go to the movies with me?" The look on Jenny's face startled him back to reality. He thought, "Holy crap! Did I just ask her out? What have I done? I blew it."

But before he could say another word, she said, "Yeah, that would be fun."

He didn't really hear her, and he backpedaled a bit, saying, "I mean, you don't have to if you don't want to. You know, I just thought it might be cool to see that new Avengers movie. But it's cool if you don't want to."

Jenny said, "Rem, did you not hear what I said? I said that would be fun."

She could sense that Remington was feeling strange in some way. Thoughts raced through her head. "Why is he acting that way? He just asked me to go to a movie. What's the big deal?"

And then it hit her. "Oh my God! He just asked me to go to a movie. Did he just ask me to go to a movie? I mean, I know he just asked me to go to a movie, but did he 'ask me out,' like on a date?" Now it was Jenny's turn to not know how to feel.

Remington said, "Uh, oh yeah, that's right. You did say that, didn't you? Okay, well, uh, what movie would you want to see?"

Jenny was lost in her own thoughts when she realized Remington had just asked her a question. "I'm sorry, Rem. What did you say?"

He replied, "I asked what movie you would like to go see."

She regained her composure and said, "I thought you just said you wanted to go to the Avengers movie. Don't you want to see that?"

"Yeah," he said. "I just didn't know if you wanted to see that one. Because we could go see something else if you want."

Jenny looked at him and smiled and said, "No, the Avengers movie sounds great." She paused and then asked, "Rem, did you just ask me out on a date?" She couldn't believe those words had escaped her mouth. She thought, "What the heck are you thinking? He finally asked you out, and you're going to put him on the spot like that and embarrass him. You idiot!"

The look on Remington's face said it all. He stammered a bit. "Uh, well, no, not really. I mean, well, you know, I just thought, it's Saturday, and there's a good movie here in town, and you know, I just got that letter from Duke, and it would be fun to go celebrate, and you know, who would I rather celebrate that with than you? So, yeah, I mean, no, it's not a date. I mean, it could be if you want it to be, but no, it doesn't have to be."

She wanted to jump across the small table and hug him and kiss him right there. He was so cute, stumbling for the words, not knowing how to handle this situation. "Oh my God," she thought. "Remington asked me out. It's happening. It's finally happening. Get your composure, and don't blow this."

Jenny put her hand out on top of the back of his hand and said, "Rem, it's me Jenny. Your best friend in the whole world. You don't have to be all flustered about this. I would LOVE to go on a date with you to the movies." She smiled the prettiest smile he had ever seen.

Remington said, "Really?!" He caught himself and said, "I mean, really? That's great. I mean, really. You'd like to go out on a date with me?"

"No," she said, and his heart sank. His expression must have shown that, too, because she quickly said, "I said I would LOVE to go out on a date with you—not LIKE to go out on a date with you." She didn't know if she should dare say the next thing that came to her mind, but there it was and out it came. "I've been waiting for you to ask me out for a long time."

"What? Really? You have?" He couldn't believe what he was hearing. "Cuz I've wanted to ask you out for the longest time, but I thought, you know, we're like best friends, and you don't think of me that way, and you know, we don't want to ruin our friendship and all."

"You've got to be kidding!" she asked. "That's exactly what I've been thinking. How long have you thought this way?"

"I don't know. Last summer. I mean, I didn't see you much because of all the camps and tournaments I was at, and I kept missing you. The more I missed you, the more I wondered why? I was so confused, but that's when I started thinking I wanted to ask you out."

"Unbelievable!" she said. "I started feeling the same way while you were gone. I'd go to work each day and think, 'When is Rem coming back from camp? Where is that tournament he's at this week?' I kept missing you, too."

They both paused, looking at each other, and smiling. Remington let out a big sigh. He said, "Wow. Imagine that. Here I was so worried about asking you out, thinking there was no way you would want that. And there you were, wishing I would ask you out, thinking there was no way I wanted that. Boy, did we blow it that last few months, huh?" He laughed.

Jenny laughed, too, and then said, "Yes and no. I mean, sure things could have been different, but then, you know, things would have been different. And this has been such a great year that maybe it was supposed to be that way. I mean, think about the season you had. If we had been, I don't know, what's the word—different—with each other, maybe things wouldn't have gone the way they did. But here you are sitting with a letter from Duke, and you're about to kick off the most important spring and summer of your basketball career. So maybe it was exactly what should have been."

"That is so like you," he said.

"Uh-oh. Is that a bad thing? What did I say?"

"NO!" he said. "No. It's outstanding. It's one of the things I love," he quickly realized what he had just said and corrected himself, "I mean one of the things I like so much about you. You can always make any situation better with how you see it and how you talk about it. You always make me feel good, make me feel like everything is going to be all right."

While she would have loved to have heard what he just said, she never heard a word after he started with, "It's one of the things I love -" She was immediately lost in her thoughts. "Did he just say he loved me? Jenny, what the heck are you talking about? He didn't say that. But he was about to say he loves certain things about me. Stop thinking that way. Get a grip."

Jenny gathered herself and said, "Well, I just try to see the possibilities in everything. And for you, I see a lot of possibilities." She paused and said, "But interestingly enough, I now see some possibilities for us, too."

Remington smiled and said, "That sounds nice. I like that." They finished their ice cream cones and got up to leave. Remington held the door open for Jenny. She walked through, and they headed towards her house. As they were walking and talking about all kinds of things, each of them was also thinking about what a great day this had been. They were also both thinking of their date that night. When they reached her house, Jenny said, "All right. Well, I'll see you tonight. What time is the movie?"

Remington had a confused look on his face. He said, "You know, I'm not even sure. I didn't even know I was going to ask you out. It just kind of happened." They laughed and he said, "I'll find out and I'll text you."

Jenny said, "Call me instead. I want to hear your voice."

Remington couldn't believe what he was hearing. It felt like his heart rose in his chest. "All right, I'll do that. You're right. That sounds better. I want to hear your voice, too. I'll call you in a little bit and let you know."

"Sounds good, Rem. See you tonight."

Remington said, "It's a date."

His words stunned both of them, and they each thought, "That's right. It's a date. I can't wait!"

Ideas to Consider:

- How is Remington one step closer to his ultimate dream?
- How does Remington's and Jenny's relationship take a new direction here? As excited as they are, what does Remington need to make sure he continues to focus on? How can Jenny help with that?

Epilogue

So, what happened? Did the Wolves work hard enough to fulfill their dreams and make it back to the state tourney, or did something trip them up along the way? Were they able to maintain their focus, their dedication, and their commitment to one another?

How did Coach Brooks and the rest of the Wolves deal with the aftermath of getting to a state tournament for the first time? Did any new problems present themselves over the course of the next year that might knock them off of their path? Will they be up to the challenge and overcome them?

Did Cade fulfill his dream of playing in college and becoming the team player he said he wanted to be? Or did he revert back to the old Cade? Did he even finish out his years as a college basketball player?

What about Remington and Jenny? That's a whole new twist that got thrown into the mix there in the final chapter. Will they take their relationship to a new level, or will their move from friends to more-than-friends be too much for their relationship to handle? Does their relationship alter Remington's trajectory to being the best player that he can be? Does it affect his college plans?

Sorry, my friends, but those are questions for another day. Answers to some of those questions and so much more await you in the future books in the Remington Roberts series beginning with the next book due out soon.

To read the next books in this series,
go to the SlamDunk Success website at:
www.SlamDunkSuccess.com.

About the Author

Scott Rosberg has served in the roles of teacher, coach, and athletic director for over 35 years. In addition to Ultimate Team Player, Scott has published multiple non-fiction books on character-based coaching and athletics, all of which can be found on his website, www.SlamDunkSuccess.com. He has also published two books of inspirational messages and quotes—one for senior athletes and one for graduates. Scott has published numerous articles, blogs, and videos on character- based coaching and athletics. He does workshops, classes, and presentations at schools, conferences, and businesses. Check out the SlamDunk Success Facebook page.

Scott is also a member of the Proactive Coaching team of speakers. Proactive Coaching is dedicated to helping organizations create character-based team cultures, while providing a blueprint for team leadership by helping develop confident, tough-minded, fearless competitors and train coaches and leaders for excellence and significance. Proactive Coaching can be found on the web at www.ProactiveCoaching.info and on the Proactive Coaching Facebook page at www.facebook.com/proactivecoach.

Other Books by Scott Rosberg

Time Out!
How We Can Fix the Problems in Kids' Sports Today

The Responsibilities of Coaching

A Head Coach's Guide for Working with Assistants

The Assistant Coach's Guide to Coaching

Playing Time:
A Guide for Coaches, Athletes, & Parents

Establishing Your Coaching Philosophy

Team & Program Policies: Elements to Consider

The Sportsmanship Dilemma:
Guidelines for Coaches, Athletes, & Parents

Building Your Coaching Staff Chemistry
eBook

Senior Salute
Gift Booklet for Senior Athletes

Inspiration for the Graduate
Gift Book for Graduates

You can find each of these titles at
www.SlamDunkSuccess.com

You can also join the SlamDunk Success community to start receiving Scott's newsletter, blog, and any new updated materials.

Email Scott with any questions at
scott@slamdunksuccess.com

Who is Remington Roberts?
Where did he come from?
How did he become such a great basketball player?

Find out in the prequel to the Remington Roberts Series—just released—*Discovery Calls: Remington Relocates.* You can get this prequel in digital format for FREE! Just go to the SlamDunk Success website and sign up to receive Scott's newsletter. You will receive a link to download the eBook, which shows you where Remington came from, where he grew up, how he started down the road to becoming a great basketball player, and how he ended up in Discovery, Montana, which is 1,100 miles away from his home.

Visit www.SlamDunkSuccess.com
and sign up for our newsletter
to get the prequel now!

Made in the USA
Middletown, DE
23 November 2022